GOD'S SKY

LESIA'S MYSTIC AND MYSTERIOUS JOURNEY

PEARL M. SMITHERN

ISBN
979-8-88945-488-5 (Paperback)
979-8-88945-489-2 (eBook)

Brilliant Books Literary
137 Forest Park Lane Thomasville
North Carolina 27360 USA

The Trip to Where

The wind did a few more twirls and twists around Lesia, making her laugh as she tried to steady herself while walking down hill, and of course, this laughter helped soothe the sadness of her heart. She thought again of what could have occurred if she had arrived earlier and had the chance to see and talk with Andrew. Lesia's mind played the game of what-if for several minutes while she kept a slow but steady pace alongside her new found friend, the lovely donkey she had named Ahava. She walked without direction, walking as in a daze.

Without realizing, Lesia began letting the little donkey take the lead. She followed because her head and her thoughts were inordinately muddled. Tired and hungry though, she knew that she needed to find another place to rest and pull herself together. (Soon she would become quite an expert in this area.) Since she had walked out on her inn job, she did not want to return there.

Ahava, with great horse sense and a gift, led Lesia to a blacksmith's hut. She knocked on his door, explaining her situation to the blacksmith and his wife, Agatha. They were more than ready to help her. Under her breath, she thanked God for this provision. Ahava too had a nice pile of straw in the shed fixed by Stan and was enjoying grain just like back at home.

Ahava and Her Story

Home, my special little barn, snuggled in the small hills of northeast of the Hypanis River, old name of river. The rivers, the greenery, the flowers, and the birds made where I was born a special place. Nadia and Bohndan Tkach were a special couple, and no donkey here on earth could have had the special care that I had. Now they are wondering why, would I have run off and not returned.

Since the Tkachs had always given me free rein at the back gate of the barn, for a few days, Nadia would just think that I had wandered off and would soon be back. What they don't know is the story behind my journey. Several months prior to the night I took off and headed out into the moonlit night, instructions were given to me from the angel.

To explain further, as a young colt, I began to realize little by little that I could understand human language, and I also began to discover that some strangeness was occurring in my ears. One day while Nadia and Bohndan were attending to my daily brushing, Nadia remarked about my ears as she stroked them in an interesting way. "She has Malka's and Aliza's ears," she told Bohndan. I don't yet quite understand that, but then I never thought that an angel would be talking to me and giving me instructions to move out of the barn late at night under the full moon so that I could see to travel and head down toward the sea. I would like to let Nadia and Bohndan in on what I am doing but this again would not be understood since she still walks in some disbelief, and sometimes when talking to Bohndan, she calls me "the strange."

From human conversation, I learned that the Apostle Andrew, the preacher man, had taken me and my grandmother, Malka, to the Tkachs when I was a young colt. Malka was a special God-sky donkey that was loved by many people, especially the children, as well as the beloved Apostle Andrew. Andrew, devoted to God and Jesus and the precious Holy Spirit, made many converts over a very large area from Scythia, Greece, to our beloved Ukraine. He was gentle and quiet, and his smile won many young ladies' hearts. Unfortunately, I too was late and missed seeing Andrew before his death on that terrible, disgraceful cross, but from what I understood, he preached to the bitter end that Christ's death on the cross was for the salvation for everyone.

Nevertheless, seeing Andrew was not my mission. I was to find a very special woman that God loved and was going to intervene in her life. She would arrive late on the death scene. My mission involved helping Lesia find her home. Yes, home to the Ukraine where Andrew gave a large part of his heart and soul preaching the love of Jesus and His salvation message. I wonder if the angel who talked to me back home saw Andrew.

The angel gave instructions for me to slip out and head down to the dock when the loading and unloading of cargo would be especially busy.

He said I would find a rich man there buying supplies as well as purchasing many horses and donkeys for his farm in Greece. He would be giving the captain a considerable amount of money to obtain a large portion of the lower part of the ship for these animals and their grain and hay. He will have also asked for another section on the ship to store his art collection, furniture, and other supplies. I was told that because of the delicateness of some items and the rarity of others that the rich man would be especially demanding. Ukraine rugs and carpets with many colorful and intriguing designs and weavings in kover, kylym, and kots styles were bought along with black smoke pottery (*horodysche-plakhtian*), pitchers (*tykva*), and bowls (*dzbanky*) with goats, rams, or stags carved into the wood. Also, packed very carefully were decorated eggs (*pysanka*).

So, the captain would make certain that this governor's wishes about this voyage and his cargo would be well attended to by the captain himself. Because of the attention given the man's other possessions, the animals would not be carefully counted. The captain will promise that all would be well and that he would deliverer the man and his lovely wife safely and soundly to Patras. I would be able to slip in easily. Upon arrival at the dock that morning, all went as the angel had predicted, and I ended up with the rest of the animals, artworks, and family to a nice farm northwest along the hillside of Patras.

One day, however, I knew with a special kind of horse sense that it was time to go, so with some strong head jerks, I broke my rope from the post at the rich man's farm and headed out toward the noise I was hearing, using the instinct of following a crowd going somewhere fast and furious. It was then that I saw Lesia slowing walking down the path and crying. She was hugging and kissing, of all things, sandals.

Mission One Completed

Ahava needed some sleep herself and like a tired, good donkey, she rolled several times over the firm grassy earth with her back. All the while with thoughts about her mission surging through her brain. Finally, she fell into sound, deep sleep, thankful for a kind old blacksmith and his wife.

Lesia

Stan and Agatha were most gracious to Lesia. When they found out that she had known Andrew from Jerusalem, they began to relate many stories to her about Andrew's visits to the area. That made the stop more special for Lesia, causing her to remember the first time she met the man she came to adore, remembering the ordeal of the fish, seeing him wet and stinking at the backdoor of Herodias's palace in Jerusalem.

Later that night, Lesia removed her belongings from her travel and placed them on the small cot in her room, thinking of how providential it was that she had learned to sew and had become such an expert seamstress that she was able to hide anything in the folds of her garments. Finally, now having the time to unstitch the hidden side of one of her scarves, Lesia pulled out the letter from Mara Chin and began to read.

Herodias my lady, greet you, Hope journey to Rome all well. Find enclosed locket Lesia as toddler. Tattered blanket gone way of old blankets. Lesia not mine. Lesia by luck became mine. Love her with all heart. Aging and customs make me scribble letter. Not take time to tell Lesia. Will soon start toward homeland. Not honorable father. No tell Lesia face to face. No want see hurt in her eyes. Break news to her, okie dokie?[1]

Also, if please, tell Lesia story. Traveling toward West from hurtful people and problems in homeland. Met Lesia's mother who begged take baby to safety. She feared for newest child. Plague was in the area; we no stay either. Mother say Lesia's older

---

[1] Means ok Funny sounding child of ok, used in story American Comedy our Gangs and Little Rascals use it. Lokie sounds like okie which means cool in Hawaiian, people with this name tend to be spiritually involved. Name Lokie also a god in Norse mythology. Mountain road in Thailand called Okidoke pass.

brother and sister would be ok. Older ones healthy. Escape danger, maybe. Honorable family agreed. Placed Lesia in wagon with younger brother's wife Acho, who wet nurse Lesia. Name little town has faded, but two rivers remembered, Borysthenes River and Hypanis River.

You show honorable daughter. She smart to trace and visit her homeland someday. Honorable family travel to Berea. Brother and wife stay. After the child weaned, took south to Athens. Heard cook needed on ship. No place for child so got off at Joppa. Remember, you visited inn in Joppa where I cooked? You asked-hire me, but I not go with you unless bring child. Was only family I had. You knew no speak truth. Also, you look at child then me. So, thank you not to open secret as long as you have. Grateful also cause shortly after we at your home, we ill. You paid doctors for us. Honorable father work for you so honorable child's ear lobe pierced-slave for life-earring. Gesture your custom.

Tell Lesia locket all that came with her. Find good heart toward her with something along with the locket.

Faithful cook and devoted servant

Lesia refolded up the letter and tucked it away. A portion of unanswered questions were answered, but even so what she had just read was unsatisfactory, not telling the whole story. She wondered why it was that she was always at the mercy of others telling her what to do and how to manage her life. She was used as a slave—a slave for life.

Mara Chin, how could you, father? she thought. Lots of emotions surfaced, first anger then love for Mara Chin for keeping and caring for her. How frightened and ill her mother must have been to give her away to a stranger—a stranger with a different lifestyle and belief system.

"Oh, mother," she silently cried. She closed her eyes and tried to picture that maybe, yes maybe, she was the image of her mother, her father, or one of her siblings. Two of them. Are they living or did they all perish in the plague?

Yes, lots of unanswered questions, but for now planning for survival is the uppermost thought in her mind; however, tonight she needed to rest then begin planning in the morning. She was more determined than ever to talk to an old sailor, any sailor, who might have information about the ships and travel. If she couldn't find someone at the wharf, she would check the small merchants and taverns. She then remembered Bishop Ben and wondered if he had found the group of Christians he was looking for. Perhaps, he had been in the crowd at the cross of Andrew. If so, she had not seen him. She was safe now from the fire in Rome, but what about her family in Ukraine? She had heard that the Ukraine was a country vast in size with many populated places. Finding her family would be searching for a small coin in a vast field. It might as well be the end of the earth for she was here in Greece, not knowing where to begin on her journey.

"Oh, Andrew, if you were alive and here to hold me in your arms, you would know just what to do," she murmured. Replacing the letter back into its secret hiding place, she stared into space and sighed a sigh that would have let everyone know how she was feeling inside her soul. But for now, she must find the strength, not to give up if she is to survive. *Yes,* she thought. *I will survive. Anyone who came out of the fire in Rome and the plague has destiny on his or her side.* But what about her family?

One part of the puzzle old Hateful knew from this letter. However, she too wouldn't have been quite sure if Lesia was Mara Chin's only child or where his homeland was located. Lesia began thinking about

Herodias. She didn't feel any ill will for her; however, neither did she have any tears for her. Herodias could have told Lesia that Mara Chin was not aging well and let her travel back to Jerusalem to see him, but she did not mention a thing about it. She only revealed that Mara Chin was attending to one of her relative's summer homes somewhere in Joppa. If he headed for his homeland, where would that be? He never talked about it.

Many long days of walking will face this tired, exhausted woman, who at this moment did not even undress or slip off her shoes but hugged Andrew's right sandal as she lay back on the old straw pillows and covered up her shoulder to sleep. The sandals unheard by her ears were in tune with heavenly secrets. Exhaustion of the day finally overcame her and soon she was fast asleep on the small cot in a dingy corner of the blacksmith's shop.

Lesia is unaware that Ahava is just like her, a traveling stranger that does not want to be left behind with another family. Only later will Lesia learn of the connection of the donkey's farm to herself.

Early the next morning the couple Agatha and Stan began to help get Lesia and Ahava ready for travel. The blacksmith checked Ahava's feet and gave Lesia a farmer's breakfast, as well as fresh fruit for her journey before she set out to approach another tavern owner. She wanted to leave Ahava there with Stan and asked if he would find a nice family for the donkey. The passage would cost more for two, especially when one was an animal. Also, what would happen if her fate would be to stowaway on the ship? Where would she hide a donkey? In addition, a major problem to consider would be if the ship captain would not take one animal. Unknown to Lesia was the fact that Ahava was in a quandary, as well. The angel didn't explain that part of the mission to her. However, the blacksmith was unaccommodating in that matter, so Ahava and Lesia left together.

The coastline was peaceful enough this morning as the seagulls circled overhead and swooped around the fishing vessels in the far distance. Lesia tied Ahava to a small bush beside the quaint tavern. Yes, this place has seen the old and the young, the good and the bad. What she didn't know was that the Good News also was a visitor here just a few months ago.

Squinting her eyes trying to look for the owner in the dim light, Lesia nearly fell over a cat. *Wow, little guy, you had better watch out for me and little old ladies*, she thought to herself. Recognition of the animal escaped her for the moment.

Hearing someone at the back doing dishes, Lesia walked toward the rear of the main room. "Humm… excuse me," she began to say when, with a startled sense of recognition, she thought that she was back in Jerusalem with Mara Chin. As the owner of the tavern turned, Lesia could not find the right words to say so just blurted out a good morning in Chinese *nizao* that she and her father had always greeted one another each morning. With a wide smile, the owner came toward Lesia, hugging her with gusto! He then began to talk in his native tongue to her, "You understand a countryman. So glad, milady. You have our greeting manners."

This was a breaking point for Lesia, and she clung to this person—a stranger to her—so closely resembling her father that her tears began to fall. He was patient and talked to her like Mara Chin did when she had been scolded by old Hateful or one of the other Roman servants. "Come, child. Sit, sit. Passion Flower tea has a calming effect. Have some ready. Yes, good. Okie dokie."

When he said that, she again stared, this time longer at his face. "The saying, where did you learn that, may I ask?"

"Oh, big brother. He talk like that. He met a sailor, and sailor taught him word. They were together on ship. He dead now I think. Have not heard from him. Tea, okie-dokie?"

"When he left on ship for Joppa, he was going to work for big person there." Bowing. "Oh, I am Lee Chin." Lisa Chin slips out of her chair as she faints away.

As Lesia slowly came to, a crowd had formed around her. Lee Chin's wife and five, stair-step children, plus three kitchen helpers were all looking down at her with perplexed, worried faces.

Tavern of Lee Chin, Her Uncle

Three months had flown by like it was only a week. Lee had a lot of ways like Mara Chin so working in the kitchen with him and his crew as one of the collective family was great therapy and her skin and her vitality was reborn. Old Hateful soon began to be just a past memory that she was determined to forget. Nevertheless, she felt each of her losses; inside she was a tender, giving human being.

In the evenings around tea time, Lesia would hear about the family's travels from so far away and how they ended up in this place. Originally, they had planned to go as far as Rome, but upon hearing of all the trouble there, they stayed awhile in Berea and then went on to Athens. Athens was much too busy for their quiet ways, so they continued their journey here to lower Patras and found work in the old tavern. An old, widow lady owned the tavern and gave the whole establishment to the Chins when she went to live with an only sister. They told the old lady that they wanted to turn the tavern into a teahouse, but she just shook her head. The old woman told the Chins how much those sailors loved their grog, but since her health was going, they could do as they wanted with this old place. However, they were told that they should be aware the place was a little bit haunted.

The old lady told many stories of all the sailors who had visited on this shore, especially the weird ones who loved to bring their pets: parrots, cats, and even rats. There was one old, one-eyed cat that came calling along with his wenching one-eyed owner. When the wenching was satisfied, they'd both be gone, so goes the story. "They would ride the ships like ghost passengers," chirped Tan as the others laughed.

Heard though, he finally got good job on a regular route, so we didn't see him as much. He left his wife and kids, they said, a mean one when crossed. "A thief if you ask me." Acho added that little bit of horror.

Remembering her voyage to Joppa, she wondered about the cat that scared Herodias. Lesia had shooed it away from the small room. Could it have been the ghost cat? She then asked about a cat that she had almost stepped on when entering the inn. "No, cat, here now," they said.

How quickly fleeting impressions floated through her mind, one minute in Jerusalem and the next back to Rome. The panic and cries which surrounded her that night sometimes still arose in her mind. She could sometimes still hear the tumult as she relived her terror while running through the streets. Who was the Roman soldier that had pulled her from the path of the chariot and fast horses? For a person in authority, he seemed to be in quite a hurry himself. Then came the search for some work in Athens, which turned out to be a little more housework than teaching children, but she was glad for Kara DeStefano and her three lovely children: Maria, Isidora, and Tomas. During her night hours, she began wondering what she was going to do with her life. Moaning within herself, she reflected upon her great love for Andrew, the inspiration to continue.

Finally, the opportunity Lesia was longing for came in the person of an elderly deacon named Bishop Ben, who stopped at Kara's home in search of more

Christians. He explained that Paul left Berea and was on his way to Athens. Paul was concerned about the church north of Berea so he had sent Timothy to the church in Thessalonica to check on them. Bishop Ben felt led to get in touch with others in Greece that may be suffering persecution, and he wanted to encourage them as Paul had encouraged him and his small group of believers. Lesia wondered where Bishop Ben was now. Did he get discouraged after seeing or hearing what happen to Andrew? Did he still want to gather more knowledge on Jesus the man that walked the shores of Galilee and was born in Bethlehem? She hoped his search did not end like hers: empty, so empty.

Searching, for what? John Mark also talked about more depth to this Jesus and his teachings. When she said, "I am enduring, Andrew," she was sincere, but now in the light of her loneliness and the emptiness of soul, enduring seemed to be a large load to bear. Lesia was beginning to feel more anger than a desire to pursue the holiness way, nor did she feel like she wanted to search out more on this new way of faith.

The noon hour was very busy at the Chin's little tavern inn. The people loved the rice along with the fish dishes that were served. The sailors who heard about Lee's cooking soon spread the word. Lesia believed that Lee Chin kept expecting the old sea goat to show up because she would catch him scanning all the customer's faces. She herself wanted this to happen then she could see firsthand instead of hearing the stories from the Chin family. The old man with a black patch; in fact, she started looking for this one-eyed man and his one-eyed cat, as well.

One evening several sailors were there to enjoy the cuisine of Lee Chin's favorite dish.

They had been aboard a merchant ship and were taking a few days to deliver goods to the locals and to some merchants. They also had brought with them some disgruntled passengers who had left Rome, looking for another place to settle. The customers lingered longer than normal to chat and swap stories. One conversation concerning Rome was very interesting. Rome had begun to try to put itself together. The talk was about how all over Rome large areas were affected politically and economically.

The extra hours spent around the tables eating and drinking that evening made a long and late night by the time the cleaning up of the serving rooms and kitchen was finished. Finally, entering her little room located behind part of the kitchen, Lesia sat down on the bed with a long, weary sigh.

Tomorrow, her thoughts raced, she wanted to go down and look at what she could find among the merchants who would be on the wharves barking their wares.

The morning came early as she was aware of Lee and his wife getting the tavern ready for another lunch and supper menu. She arose and this time after she dressed, she approached Lee. "Uncle Lee, I would like to go down to the dock and look for some things to buy. I did not pay the blacksmith and his lovely wife for all they did for me and my donkey, and if I find some things, I want to go back up and visit them. May I beg off for the day?"

"Ah, sure, little blossom, go and Tan will help in your place." He smiled a smile that sent a special remembrance of Mara into her heart.

Slipping back into her room, she removed a small, wrapped cloth pouch. Inside its lining, she loosened a stitch and pulled out a small piece of jewelry, one that would not bring a lot of money but enough and would not give her away as some very rich woman. She desired to also buy some herbs for Lee Chin, herbs like Mara, who could afford them, had used in his cooking for old Hateful. These herbs would enhance her uncle's dishes and the added flavor would increase his business. Some new teas, as well, like Pomegranate, Cranberry, and Echinacea would also help in the menu.

Donkey's Thoughts

Ahava, already sensing the adventure of getting away from the tavern, could almost hear the noise down by the sea. Heading toward the big wharves where little boats were tied up and viewing the incoming bigger ships docked further out in deeper water reminded her of the midnight miracle walk she had accomplished in getting on with the God-sky mission.

What would Lesia find to her liking? "Maybe, she could get me an apple." Back home on the farm when Bohndan thought his animals were hungry for an apple, he would bring a bagful, but Ahava's apple would always have a flaw. Bohndan would invariably take a few bites out of it first.

Ahava wondered how her far away family were faring, missing them suddenly and yet beginning to bond with this aging woman who was now flowing with vitality. Ahava had begun to learn many things about Lesia in the short time they had been together. She noted Lesia's great love for Andrew and that she had not fallen in love with any other man, nor had she mentioned anything about desiring marriage. Ahava also noticed that Lesia had a good heart, but was also showing some anger at the turn of events in her life. She thought Lesia must be wondering what else she would find out about herself. Unknown to Lesia is Ahava's mission and where she originally came from. However, soon Lesia will find out more, but for now she only thinks of Ahava as a donkey from the farm in Greece. *Oh, how I wish that angel was here right now. I need to do more than to just eat grass and keep watch, and right now my ear is twitching. Human actions would be appreciated*, Ahava thought, switching her tail back and forth as she clomped alongside of Lesia.

People of all sizes and shapes were talking and soon the sound was a little too much for Ahava's ears. She jerked away and headed toward an open space near a bench by some trees.

"Oh, Ahava, there you go again acting different."

Different, another description of me, again, thought Ahava. *If Lesia only knew how all this noise was scrambling my hearing. Well, anyway, I shall enjoy some green grass and tune it out.*

An hour went by like it was a few minutes as Lesia enjoyed the bartering and rebartering, making the memories of her courtyard experience alive again as when she would go to get things for Mara Chin and old Hateful. "Father, are you really gone from my life?" Shaking off these thoughts, she became aware of a small, dirty, hungry, thin child wrapped closely in a tight bundle on a mother's back. She swallowed slowly and stared and pondered why, how, or should she care. Then suddenly, she remembered Andrew's face and his kind eyes, as well as his remarks about how the disciples once tried to stop children from coming to Jesus and Jesus had scolded them. Andrew observed that Jesus loved them. In fact, He explained that heaven is for children or was it that people had to be like a child. "I can't remember, Andrew. Andrew, right now I do miss you and am so sad inside, but I will go on. So, Andrew, my love, for you and for your Jesus, I am going over to have a talk with that young woman and try to help even if she doesn't want it."

The young woman responded quickly with her story, seeing she had a consoling one open to her story; thus, she elaborated, fully stating that her family was destroyed by the fire in Rome. Since she was poor, nobody cared about her, so with what she had left, she purchased a ticket and got on board the ship. Now standing, she bewailed, "I feel so lost," and at that moment, the tears flowed freely.

Lesia wrapped her arms around the young mother and the baby and whispered, "You are safe now. I want you to join me and be a part of my family, for you see, I am a lonely woman who has been looking for my love and my connections—my birthplace. So, you see, we can be a comfort to each other, and besides, having never married or had children, I would love helping with your little one. But you don't have to give me an answer right now. I want you to just go to the tavern of Lee Chin and tell them Lesia sent you. I have to take some things to the blacksmith's wife, and then I will be back and we will continue the discussion of how we are going to approach, yes, approach life and living together." And at that Lesia hugged the young woman again, and both laughed as "Misery loves company" silently ran through both their minds.

The young lady had one extra laughable thought, *This woman believes my story.* As she turned to go on her way, she tossed her hair to one side, a pleased expression on her face, thinking, "Paula, you could be an actress."

Just then, Ahava caught the scent of a strange odor coming from the bundle. She realized that the child might be sick, really sick. This new awareness—illness was a new and deeper[2] supernatural awaking, and she shook herself and walked quickly away from the woman and her child. Ahava followed Lesia, who moved hurriedly to finish her errands and deliver the things to the blacksmith family for she was anxious to return to the Lee Tavern and to the unknown young woman and boy child.

Paula LaRosa

Paula LaRosa stood for a few minutes trying to realize what had just happened to her, a stranger dumped off a ship with a hidden pouch, but now she had a place to go to for food and shelter for the night. She had met a tall, beautiful stranger, a kind woman to travel with, who was also willing to help with the baby boy.

Paula walked into the tavern where the smell of food and wine mingling with happy voices was too much to handle. Being so weak herself, she had no sooner entered through the door before she fell to her knees again letting her tears flow. Bathing her face gently with soft cloth, Mrs. Chin remarked to her

---

[2] When the Supernatural Handiwork of *God Keeps You*. PS.19

husband, "I hope, love one, that this is not a relative, also. Hee, hee."

Paula blurted out then that while at the wharf a beautiful lady gave her instructions to come to this inn and wait for her return from her errand at the blacksmith's farm. "Yes, yes." Lee Chin nodded as he motioned for his wife to take the baby while he helped the young lady back to Lesia's room at the very back of the tavern. Paula then asked if she could have some milk for the baby. "I have no milk," she told them.

Startled, Lee Chin prepared some diluted goat's milk in a clay jar for the mother.

Leaving the room, Lee Chin whispered to his wife that he believed that the baby seemed very ill. He wanted to say something to the mother but decided to wait for Lesia. "Lesia will do something, okie dokie, husband," Mrs. Chin whispered back.

Paula folded diapers from several pieces of cloth Mrs. Chin had brought back to the room along with a pitcher of water, some clean cloths, old towels and bedding and some gowns that Tan had outgrown. She took a diaper and after a few minutes got the child changed, feeling that its skin was warmer than it was before at the wharf, a boy child taken from a mother who was too ill to object. She was probably dead by now. Stolen, yes, but merchant ship's captain charged a lower fare for a mother and child leaving Rome. "How was I going to know that this woman with a baby would collapse right before my eyes before boarding?" Opportunity is what counts now some days, and Paula took it.

So easy, so easy. The baby made the fare cheaper and was a blessing for her. Paula felt the tiny one's head. "Could this be something bad? Was this what was wrong with its mother? Now will I get sick? Will, I infect this whole family?" Paula looked around the room for a place she could place the infant child. She was also considering the future. If the baby wouldn't make it through the night, Paula would be out the door. The baby wasn't hers, so why should she care? Didn't life make her an orphan now along with being an abused woman who had to enjoy the favors of men, especially one soldier in Rome? Also, the woman at the wharf believed the so sorry routine. She was an easy target if there ever was one. Paula smiled. So far, this baby has brought two blessings. If there is no baby in the morning, then she will have to use her wiles to exist. Men are men everywhere.

Blacksmith's Home

Ahava was a blessing because she remembered just where the little blacksmith's hut was located alongside the small cottage called home. Seeing that the day was well spent, Lesia realized that the visit will have to be short indeed. As they arrived back at the blacksmith's home. Ahava took off toward for the back of the shed. She needed a good roll because her back was asking for it.

"Come in, come in. Oh, how well you look. It seems that our weather and climate have suited you very favorable," Agatha giggled out, along with a strong hug. "You, my dear child, are just in time for our early supper because Old Ben is here too to say goodbye."

Old Ben, recognizing Lesia, stood and greeted her also. "I am so glad to see you." Lesia then shared her story about seeing Andrew and what it all meant. Ben informed her that he had not seen Andrew's death but it was the talk of the fellowship. He explained to them how that the Christian groups he found were still mourning the loss of Apostle Andrew but were vowing to keep his teachings. They certainly now strongly believed in the Man called Jesus. Andrew's death made them recognize that this faith he taught is what brings man a happy life on earth, in addition to the knowledge of a heaven to gain. "The people have decided to continue with their plans to build a church and give it Andrew's name. I am sure from their determination, and with the help of God, it will get accomplished."

What a dinner. Agatha was certainly a good cook, thought Lesia. "Agatha, sometimes my Uncle Lee needs help in his kitchen, and since you are a natural cook, have you ever thought of working outside the home? If so, please come help my uncle. He will pay you well."

Thanking Lesia for the extra spices and tea, Agatha mentioned that it would be good for her and Stan can shoe horses down at the wharf. That would bring in extra income for both, and Agatha would have a safe journey down to that area. Smiling, along with receiving more hugs from Agatha, who was truly a woman with a very warm soul, Lesia prepared to go. Lesia thought from all the hugging and giving of food. *No wonder her name means good and kind.*

Next, Ben gave Stan and his wife his gracious thanks and told them that his whole visit to this area had been delightful. He too had a long trip ahead, and since he was heading back the same way, he would escort Lesia, taking of course some extra vitals to store in his knapsack. Lesia wanted to ask if she could go back to Athens and then further north with him, but then thought of the lady and a baby that could be sick. They were still too fresh on her mind so leaving right now was out of the question.

Ben, Lesia, and Ahava were all very quiet as they walked back toward the tavern down near the busiest wharves in Patras. Lesia extended her invitation for Ben to spend the night and meet her Uncle Lee, who came through Berea years and years ago with her father. She knew that her uncle would not turn him away. "It is custom," Mara would say, "to show good manners to a guest, so arrange slippers carefully by side door after brushing them. You also prepare good tea for travel. It is a body resting herb. Okie dokie?

Entering the tavern, she could see that the sailors loving her uncle's tavern were again going to make it a long, long night. She kissed her uncle on the cheek, bowed, and quickly headed to her room to redress and begin to help in the dining and kitchen area.

Upon going into her room, Lesia saw that the young woman and the child were fast asleep on the end of her small bed. She tiptoed over to cover them up, glancing again at the baby, who was now looking a little flushed. She touched its brow. "Oh no. Fevered."

But with the noise of Acho Chin in kitchen saying, "Coming, I am coming. Hurry best I can. Food hot, be careful please." Lesia hurriedly changed her blouse for her long white one and put on the white apron then turned and headed toward the kitchen. She was just in time to take a tray of food from her aunt for the group in the left side of the room. The aroma of cooking began mixing with the smell of the night air, of chewing tobacco, and of smoke from the lamps.

Lee Chin and Ben were still in conversation as the last tea cup was hung and the floor brushed with his makeshift wide broom, a very good one. Lee Chin also had the ancient gift of making things. The weaved baskets and art pieces made from clay, painted in pretty, and bright colors made the atmosphere seem like the culture of the Far East mixing in with the smell of tobacco and the blown-out lamps, giving the tavern an eerie but warm glow, for right now, it was empty of all the customers except for those in the far-right corner table.

Ben was explaining the Good News to Lee Chin, the gospel being taught over a widespread area with many becoming Christians because of the risen Jewish man that died by the Roman method of crucifixion in Jerusalem. Ben also told Lee about the believers that Andrew had won here in Patras, and how badly they felt that some of their friends on the council headed up by the one unbelieving Governor helped in having him executed.

The day has drawn to an end. Did Lee Chin receive this Gospel news? Lee Chin beds himself down beside his wife's bed on the floor so as not to disturb her. Ben is in silent prayer as he beds down beside a very nice donkey. The tavern soon was totally silent as night settled, a small fog forming ready to slip in toward early morning hours. What was not seen was a small mouse being chased through the back entrance by a one-eyed cat.

Lesia entered as quietly as she could into the small room. She slipped out of her shoes and gently rubbed her aching feet. Andrews's sandals were lying by the side of the dresser because she usually slept with one, but during the last few months, she had left that ritual alone. Why tonight were they tugging on her mind? Dismissing the thought, she slipped into her long, granny nightgown and rearranged the two extra blankets down alongside of the small cot as best she could without lighting a candle. Glancing at the sleeping child and its mother, the penetrating sound of a small whimper could be heard. She knew it was coming from the suffering child.

Rising on her elbows, she then went to her knees and gently slipped the child down onto her blankets, feeling the radiating hotness of the baby's skin. What to do? Should she wake the household? Would Uncle Lee and Acho know what to do? As she slowly moved her body on her knees and tried to balance herself into an upright position, she fell to the right alongside a small trunk where she had placed Andrew's sandals. Then in the dark she smelled the sweet aroma of his sandals. She froze and then reached for one of them. "Andrew, Andrew," she whispered, "what if this was our little boy?" Without thinking, Lesia placed the sandal behind the child's back and lifted her heart in a sincere prayer as she rocked back and forth for a few minutes, contemplating on what she should do. What she wasn't aware of was that for the remainder of the night the few minutes she spent with the sandal and the brief prayer for the goodness of the anointing of God initiated the work of Andrew's sandals on the sickness of the small baby boy and gave a God-sky sleep hug to a tired, lovely woman greatly loved.

With morning approaching, Paula awakened and looked around the small room. How could she have fallen so deeply into a sleep to not have been aware of her surroundings? She knew she must not do that when on her own in this world. She is, after all, street smart, not stupid. On the floor, at the foot of the cot she noted the lovely woman snuggled down with both arms around a beautiful, wiggling baby boy who had kicked off blankets, and had a sandal on its foot.

She with a puzzled look had to look again. The baby boy was a beautiful child. Her first thought was that the fever broke, which meant that she had escaped a serious disease of some sort but now arose the problem of how to deal with a naive, sincere woman.

Lesia, awaking to the banging of the loudest pots and pans in the kitchen, looked up with surprise and greeted Paula, and with an, oh my, felt something warm against her body. At that moment both women went into action. Lesia had not even noticed that the sandal had fallen off to the side of the blankets. Once more it had become just an ordinary sandal.

Paula showed Lesia the things that Acho had brought in for her to use for herself and the baby.

Lesia then revealed that she would be bringing in a small tub for both to use for bathing. A good bath would make anybody feel like living. Holding the baby out to get a good look at him and feel his head with her lips, she smiled and said, "Oh my, my dear, I forgot your first name."

"My name is Paula."

"Well, Paula, the baby's fever seems to have gone away. It was probably just caused by his teeth. I need to hurry to help uncle and start the water boiling, so you wait here awhile, and I will be back." Lesia reflected on her ability to hurry, thinking about Herodias's bath time.

Anthony Rom

The legends of the founding of Rome, based upon a wolf for a mother, gave rise to its first king, Romulus. Many more kings follow, but like in most countries, through time records could be lost. The pride of the people continued though, and with the various kings, diverse groups were formed to help in governing; however, the groups were designed to carry out the kings wishes. They believed that their king was connected to the gods and looked upon their leader from a religious viewpoint. Kings, as head of the state, were the only ones who were permitted to wear the purple toga and the white diadem on their heads. As Rome conquered more territory and became increasing enlarged it began to be known as the Roman Empire, which reigned from 27 BC to AD 1453.

Anthony loved his Rome, and even under the complication of Nero as ruler, he held a very high position as second to the commander of the Roman Military. The military was organized into legions, with appointed military leaders to manage the wars, yet was always under the authority of the current ruler of Rome.

Anthony's father sat in the Senate, and many times he told Anthony in secret that Nero was given good advice about how to rule the empire effectively, but he had his own views, especially about Christians. He ignored valuable suggestions that later came an impediment to his rule. One such action was in the killing of his own mother.

July 19, AD 64, the six-day fire. Anthony and his father rode silently as they went to see what areas were damaged by the fire. Tacitus told them that only four of the fourteen districts escaped the fire. As they viewed the damage, they noted that three of the districts were completely ruined, while seven others were so badly damaged as to make them unlivable. They observed workmen carrying away the marble that could be saved for use in Nero Domus Transitoria's new palace, Domus Aurea. They spoke of the Nero's blame casting and how Christians, guilty or innocent, were to be covered with skins of beasts and then set upon by dogs. Others had been nailed to crosses while still others were doomed to flames that served as nightly illuminators at Nero's palace at sundown.

Anthony turned to his father and began to voice his disgust. "This is it, Father. I have followed orders that were for the pride of war and conquest, but to human disgrace, no, this is as much as a man can endure. Recently, a fellow soldier, my friend, came back from Jerusalem and told me what he was involved in there. He was instructed to help crucify a Jewish teacher, who was called the King of the Jews. When he returned to Rome, the first thing he did was to resign his commission, just to find himself dishonored and a joke of the service. He watched as his family was carried away to prison, maybe to death—death to Christians. Then Nero's only thought is to build a bigger and grander palace. I have lost respect for him and for his leadership over our countrymen."

"I have already sent Margaret and our child to our summer villa in Patras. She needed to get to a dryer climate, and the smoke inhalation did not help her condition. I hereby turn in my resignation with, I hope, your approval, and ask that your voice be raised to persuade the senate to agree. Margaret is feeling ill, and I am full of shame."

Anthony and his father begin to gallop faster now toward his father's home. Upon arrival, Anthony Rom shook his head and hit his chest, as he habitually did in honor and respect toward country and father then dismounted from his lovely mount Pegasus. She was fair and slender with racing legs that ran like the wind. "Here, Father, take her and let no one say I took anything from the stables of the Roman Empire. If the Senate finds my record was honorable, may the gods of Romulus let me have my horse. You, Father, are an upright man and well respected in the Senate. May our gods favor the change of protocol for me when you ask about me leaving the tribunes."

Kissing his father, who pledged he would get the Senate to handle some of the injustice and see about his friend's family, Anthony went on his way. When Anthony arrived at his own villa to see about its damage, he found he was without any remnant of his former life. This time no one ran out to hail him as a great warrior. Margaret and his baby son were by now very safe and sound in their summer cottage in Patras.

Ready to set sail, Anthony turned to go to the wharf to join his wife and son in Patras. While walking down the road, however, he was met by a burial group. "What have we here, friends?"

"A woman, your wife," they replied.

"No, you have got to be in jest. My wife and son were to set sail for Patras this morning." Throwing back the blanket, he discovered that it was indeed his lovely Margaret, but there was no body of the child. Even though he was a well-trained soldier of the empire, second in command when needed, he now found that his bravery deserted him as he lifted the lifeless body of his wife, hugged her to his bosom one last time, and wept.

Gathering his wits, Anthony slowly asked how his wife had died and why was his son not with them. His friends told him that the captain found Margaret collapsed on the gangplank during the process of loading the ship, and that her lady-in-waiting took the child on ahead. "Lady-in-waiting? We have never had such women in our employment." Now he was overcome with anguish and fear.

Anthony took Margaret to his father's household and placed her into the family crypt. Then a change came over Anthony's countenance and his heart, a change including the desire to kill. His life seemed to be collapsing around him: the love of his wife gone, the honor of his country in tatters, the child of his love, abducted. "I will find our precious child and the heartless woman who took what was not legally hers, a helpless child along with my love's money pouch."

The weather was rainy, which fit his darkened mood. All in his father's household could see that he was a man with a mission. With the sharp words of a trained leader and fire in his eyes, he bid farewell to father and servants and set out toward the sea.

The docking at Patras's wharf was simple enough. Now standing on the dock, Anthony was empty of feelings, but he kept examining all who were about—man, woman, or child—looking for anyone who may have taken his child. He stood there with a heart-wrenching numbness. Margaret was gone, a kind, laughing wife who endured his hours away to serve. To serve, and on that note, he spits on the ground and cursed Rome.

Then he headed toward his small cottage up in the hills of Patras's quiet countryside. Where once was joy, remembering his honeymoon, his marriage, but now death. There he would be facing the world of singleness once again.

When Anthony arrived at the cottage, he aired out the rooms, hearing the refreshing sound of the morning wind rushing throughout each corner of the small cottage, removing the heat and dusty smell that had accumulated from days of closed doors in a locked-up cabin. His exhaustion overwhelmed him in his grief and sleep was a blanket of comfort for now as he crashed upon his bed, glancing toward the corner where his sword and a small knife rested, the only part left of his soldier's outfit and Rome.

Next morning, Anthony awakened with surprise to a favorite thrill of the birds chirping forth their joy of the morning. Sleep had helped, but what to do now and where to begin faced him directly as he contemplated his future. Aware of the emptiness of his stomach, he first wanted to awaken his body, drawing up water from the cistern outside. Even though the water was cold, he was glad for its jarring effect. A trained soldier shunned the soft, easy life to stay tough, ready, and alert.

What irony. No one was ready for Rome to burn, and he was not ready to face his love's breathing issues arising from the odor of burning iron gates and debris.[3]

Together the decision was made that she would leave for Patras, going to a climate where the fresh air would help heal her asthmatic spells. Anthony would follow as soon as he could get a discharge or permission from the Senate for a leave of absence. His father had great respect among the men of the Senate, and they knew of Anthony's need to be with his ailing wife. Also, there was the child to consider. It was a simple plan. He had kissed Margaret goodbye

---

[3] Information from Great Fire of Rome

and rode off to meet his father to inspect the ruins of Rome, giving Rome one last duty before getting his departure papers. Then personal disaster struck.

When the men brought Margaret to him, he contemplated— duty to Rome or duty to find his child? He knew he made the correct choice, for what were his goals and dreams compared to his love for his child. In addition, he had become more and more infuriated with Rome's disintegration from a moral high point into raucous living for pleasure alone. He dressed and headed toward the blacksmith's home, his nearest neighbor.

Agatha had just finished bringing in fresh eggs from the hen-house, while Stan was cleaning out the stables and rubbing down the black beauty of a stallion that he boarded for Anthony Rom of the house of Claudius. Chores done, they kissed each other as they both talked over the events of the day while working on a good breakfast. They spoke about Bishop Ben and Lesia and discussed the possibility of working some days down at the seashore and at Lee Chin's tea tavern.

The firm, hard knock on the door startled the two who said, "What in the world!" Opening the door, there stood Anthony both bid him welcome and Stan said, "Friend, I was just thinking about you when I fed your King." Setting another plate, they both learn the plight and heartache of a couple whose wedding they had celebrated years ago. They were aware of the burning of Rome from Lesia and others who had moved to Patras to find new living places. But Anthony's wife's death and missing child caused the kitchen to grow quiet as they let him continue. "I need my horse."

"King has just been fed and recently reshod. Also, he had a good run and is in fine condition. The saddle is where you left it." Shaking his head, he said, "No, no. Don't worry about what you owe me. Just come back and leave King again if you must, but for all that is holy, may God speed you to find your baby boy."

Thinking over recent events, Stan told Anthony that the only new lady they have met was Lesia who came from Rome to Athens; and then she and Bishop Ben traveled to Patras together. "Lesia's Uncle Chin runs the tea tavern outside of town. Maybe they might have some news or have seen someone with a young child." Agatha, being who she was, quickly took left over cheese and small cakes, sealed them in a bag, and handed them it to Anthony.

"A saint you are Agatha," he said, giving her a swift hug. He then hit his chest and turned toward the door and down to the blacksmith's stable.

He just let King have his head and run as swiftly as he desired, giving Anthony an uplifting, soul-filling moment, feeling free again, young again. But the moment was short-lived and as King slowed down, Anthony's thoughts returned to the important pursuit in his life. He viewed again this lovely countryside, loved by them both, a place where his son could have had the best of everything.

Lee Chin's Tavern

Bishop Ben surprised about his sleeping companion for the night, slept well, and upon waking, discussed his travel plans. First, he wanted to return to Athens and then see about a ship sailing toward the small islands close to Ephesus where he could visit with Timothy. He heard some news that the apostle John had taken Jesus's mother Mary to Ephesus, and he wanted to check this out. He would then decide if he would make the long journey back to Berea on foot. It certainly would be cheaper to travel this way, but more importantly, traveling by foot would give him the opportunity to spread the Good News Gospel message along the way. He felt stronger in his calling since the group in Patras laid hands on him, praying for him to continue as a follower and believer in Jesus Christ, strengthening him to spread the message along the way. The apostle Paul had motivated him to serve in this capacity when Paul had preached in Berea and Andrew's preaching further strengthened his desire to spread the Good News. Traveling expenses could be earned by chopping wood or other small jobs to earn money for the journey.

Yes, he thought, *he would help people along the way, starting now with Lesia.*

Lesia listened to Ben then knew in her heart that he was God's provision sent to assist her in her endeavors to find her birthplace. She wanted to locate the river where Lee and Mara Chin first encountered her as a babe and took her with them on their journey. Yes, this would also help with her expenses for the journey and be a safer way to go. With her teaching or sewing skills, she could also help earn along the way. Neither knew what God had in His plans for both.

Lesia came in and approached the group. "Ben. Ben, you are not going alone. Please take us with you. She told them that she must also leave to continue her quest to find her kinsmen. She expressed her love and devotion to her Uncle Lee Chin, but inside, her heart was longing to find her beginnings, an unheard calling so to speak."

Paula listened to everything that was said. To go with them or stay was her dilemma. If she stayed, how was she to earn money? It would be hard work or the lady's night card. The baby's cry disrupted all the talk, and Lesia rushed back to the bedroom. Paula soon followed and took the baby from Lesia's arms, laying him down again to tend to his diaper. Lesia watched as Paula bent over the infant. Paula's dark black hair matched the child's perfectly. She talked softly to him as she changed him, and the baby responded. Lesia thought, *How could this child have become mine? What a foolish thought. A child belongs to his mother.*

Paula was thinking her own thoughts. She had heard of Athens, but most of all, she thought of the new city, Alexandra of Egypt, which was growing daily as her Egyptian jailer in Rome bragged one night. "Yes, how ironic. I will get free help to Athens then dump this kid and miss holy, good shoes. Bishop Ben might be holy, but he took a look or two. But for now, it is time to go into act three."

"You all have been like my family, so please take me and my child with you. Please, I have no one," and on that note, Lesia was more than glad, for she was drawn to the child more than the mother. But no mother, no child, so she was quick to say, "Of course, Paula, you are going. Did I not tell you at the dock that I am without anyone also and that we can be of help to each other?" So, the night was joyous like a last supper with the Lee Chin family. Plans were to be early on the road with Ahava packed down good and heavy.

Ben remarked though, "I believe your donkey has grown some." *Yes*, thought Ahava, glad for the Spanish mix[4] in the blood line, thinking that her visitor in white neglected to mention her role in being a beast of burden.

The journey was long but without incident. On the last day of travel, the miles went by quickly because Ben kept a good gait along with Ahava, and the idea of getting there before sunset was a great incentive to not slacken the walking pace. Lesia remarked that her employer lived just outside of the big city, and she felt sure Kara would welcome them in for the night.

Mrs. Kara DeStefano and the three children were extremely surprised but glad to see her again. She was the kindest one of the tutors they had but they only realized her value when she had moved on. Ben, Paula, and the baby all were welcome.

Bishop Ben left to go down to check out the shipping routes and to inquire about getting a horse and wagon. He found a goat and brought her back so

---

[4] Andalusian strong and sturdy breeds

it would supply baby milk. Kara provided them with an iron pot, a few pans, and a small barrel that would be very useful to carry water.

The children were smitten with the baby. They also were drawn to the donkey. The adults kept hearing laughter and lots of chattering from the children outside. Lesia wondered what they found so fascinating about Ahava, her donkey, yet sometimes Ahava had acted differently.

Differently, indeed, one of the three children had a speech problem, and Ahava knew this. Tommy[5] would look up at Ahava and mouth his childlike fascination to pet her right ear. When it vibrated in the child's hand, Tommy's eyes grew big and out came a good sound from the lips of a stuttering child. "Donkey ears wiggles," said the child, and his sisters understood his speech. He said it again. They kept watching Tommy grabbing Ahava's right ear and noticed how his speech kept getting clearer just from touching the animal even by petting her nose. Then Ahava lowered her head so that the child could again repeat the miracle in progress. When the adults arrived, the children grew quiet because who would believe what they had just witnessed.

---

[5] Greek name; Tommy(Tomas)

Paula took the baby and went back to another smaller room to change his diaper and be in ear shot of what Lesia and Ben are planning. She began doing some soul searching as to where she wanted to live. In her heart, she scoffed at going north. They were not her people, her kind. She wanted to live in a more active city like the one she was born in, Rome. She thought of the island of Crete and the land of Egypt. South, she decided, was where she wanted to go for her future. She looked at the child. "Should I take you for a meal ticket, little one, or should you stay with Miss Holy Good Shoes? You are a cutie and that smile surely makes me think your father was one handsome man. I know one thing for sure; you are definitely Roman with that nose.

Looking around the luscious room, she mused, "Hmm…nice small candleholders, looks like they might be gold." She slipped them down into her bag. She then heard Drew, as Lesia started calling him, whimper. It was getting close to feeding time. She decided to let him fuss a little for now, but little did she realize that this child was growing inside her stony heart. The loss of her baby boy was a nail that had shut her heart! The guard had informed her, "I am so sorry, but your little boy did not make it."

Heart, let Jesus come into your heart. Paula had heard enough of the Jesus and your heart. She noticed that Lesia always hung on to every word Bishop Ben said about the Good News and a future in a new heaven. "I go to prepare a place for you," was often quoted by Ben. But she wondered what they knew of the heart and the place where that guard laid her baby.

Paula mused, my life was young and carefree back in Rome, then father died fighting for the cause of the Empire, and mother started slipping away to the catacombs. Paula's mother had met Peter's wife, Anna who initiated change in her behavior and soon Paula began to go with her, as well. She had a young mind and heart and was so eager to know about the world so going to hear Peter was exhilarating, plus the secrecy was always a challenge.

As she continued to look around the room, Paula further contemplated about her past. She had thought that Peter was a good man; however, his end proved what she thought about the Gospel message, it ended in death not life. Life was what she kept in her heart. She remembered the night they were raided. The authorities knocked over the tables and shackled all who they could get their hands on. They claimed it was for Rome, mocking the Christian gathering, stating that Nero is god here.

Paula was grabbed by her hair. The brute who grabbed her told the others, "This one's a beauty. Can't let the beast tear such a delicate specimen. "She's mine, Gaius," yelled to the others as he put his own shackle around her neck. "Yes, she will bring in a pretty silver tetra drachma."

"My mother's honest and gracious life. What did my lovely mother do to Rome? Father gave his life for the growth of the Empire. He always said, 'We conquer; we are blessed by our gods.' Right. Now rubbish to Rome and her gods and to whatever Rome stood for and now rubbish to these Christians. I want no part of it or this Jesus," Paula pondered aloud.

At this, little Drew whimpered louder. Rushing to the kitchen, Paula realized that the child who was tongue-tied was watching her. "Move, child, shoo." He quickly darted out of the kitchen. Grabbing the whole skin-bag full of milk and taking the small knife from the center counter, she rushed back to the baby. "Shhhh…little one," Paula whispered, giving him enough milk to bring silence. She gathered a few more baubles and fixed the knife in a hiding place. Silently, she began to creep out of the room to head toward the stone garden and the small gate in back.

Pulling back the blanket, Paula rechecked Drew, noting that he was still clutching his favorite toy,

Andrew's right sandal. Halfway down the path, the child let out a small whimper, but then he settled once more. He fell asleep again, while the music of God from the unseen world played—the same music that Andrew heard.

Lesia

The stuttering child had taken a dislike to the younger woman. He knew she was up to something when she took all the milk. Returning to the adults after Paula's harsh get out, he tried to get his mother's attention, but his small voice was not even noticed as he tugged on his mother's skirt. "Go play, child," she said, "Go on, honey, join the others outside with Ahava." He approached his siblings, joining in with their fun, thus losing what he saw for a moment when he again pulled on Ahava's ear.

Bishop Ben kept going over their various options, trying to decide the best route. Of the ships sailing out today, only the one going to the island of Crete would be helpful, but not the best choice. It would then travel on to Cairo and Alexandria, Egypt. Tomorrow, there was a ship coming in from Joppa that would then go up to Miletus.

"I know of a widow who runs an inn. We could stay awhile with her and then decide our next move."

"What do you think, Lesia?"

"Yes," Lesia said, remembering her sore feet after the four-day walk from Patras to Athens, "the ship would lessen the amount of walking. Water voyage seems more appealing. But, Ben, I thought you wanted to go back to Berea. Oh, Ben, what about Ahava?"

"Now quit fretting, child. The ship that is coming in is a merchant ship, and it can carry and handle animals. Let's get us a good supper and leave at the first morning light. Kara can have the wagon I purchased to use around here for her and the children, so nothing is a loss to me."

Finally, Lesia headed toward the back of the house made into a makeshift bedroom for her and Paula. She burst into the room calling out, "Paula, Paula." No answer, turning around in a complete circle, she felt her heart beating faster and faster but only encountered silence. Looking quickly round for Andrew's right sandal, gone, she felt like someone kicked her in the chest as she let her joy turn into gloom from Hades. Then she went to check that smaller room closer to the main room. "What? Oh, no! How could I have trusted Paula? She was acting withdrawn, but I thought it was from all the religious talk in front of her." Then in walked the small, speech-impaired child, and in his small voice, he said clearly, "Mean lady took baby!" Lesia fell to her knees. Her Drew and Andrew's right sandal were gone.

No one knew much about the real Paula or her trauma in the catacombs the night she was taken prisoner. Now the supper table was quiet indeed. Earlier, when Kara heard Lesia crying, she and Ben had rushed back to see what was the matter. Upon hearing the story, Kara soon realized that Paula was more than a runaway, she stood looking at the missing spots where candles sat. She was also a thief.

Anthony Rom

Anthony's outing on king was cathartic, what doctors would call a blood leeching. "Ha."

He threw his head back and was now on a mission. "I should have been not as abrupt with my gracious neighbor, always nice, but a soldier is what I am. Now don't worry, Margaret my precious love, I shall find our child," he said, choking on that thought. *Our child*, it hit him hard and a tear was wiped aside by the wind on his face—his son! Margaret and Anthony couldn't have children, so she never knew about his affair. She thought that Anthony had saved the babe from death when his parents were killed because they were Christians.

They were going to have him blessed by Zeus and then name him after his father and King Lucius Superbus.

Margaret's sister lives in Athens and is unaware that her sister has died and that the child has been taken. Revenge fills his heart at the thought of this travesty. Even though he doesn't have a clue as to what this woman looks like, how old she is, or how he is going to find her, his mission is to find his child and administer justice. Anthony's anger had become aroused to the point that King was beginning to foam at the mouth. Noticing now what he was doing, he quickly dismounted and wiped King's mouth, uttering comforting words to him while walking along side of him. He realized too that he had come halfway past a portion of the wharves where some of the ships were docked, and entering another part of the wharf where merchants were selling wares. His problems and anguish were oblivious to him to all around, except for his faithful horse who knew his master was troubled!

Anthony looked at the rustic inn in comparison to his father-land home. The inn stood in great contrast, just a small hole in the wall was Lee Chin's tea tavern. Some shrubs placed around, a horse pole for customer's mounts, a wider place for carts, and lovely flowers arranged like they were specially placed by a thoughtful gardener's hands. Wiping his feet as he'd been trained to do, he entered the inn. As his eyes adjusted to the dimness, he noted that the room looked larger than what it appeared to be on the outside. He scanned the room and noticed that sea sailors, the primary customers, were all enjoying the Greek and Oriental cooking aroma of their forthcoming food.

Tan Chin approached him. "Sir, want table? Yes, okie dokie, follow me." Anthony did and seated himself with his back to the wall and his face toward the door.

"Young man, may I speak to the owner of this tavern, perhaps your father?

"Yes." Tan bowed and left to get Lee.

Lee bowed and smiled. "I know from your presence you are a Roman soldier, Welcome and how may I serve you."

Anthony motioned with his hand for Lee to sit down. He cleared his throat and noticed the kindness of this man facing him and soon the whole story was explained. Lee's facial expression dropped, and his eyes grew teary, a direct signal to Anthony that Lee knew. He knew something; he had seen his son! Lee quickly went to the back and got his wife. Then they both explained how Lesia found Paula with a sick child.

"Now man, where are they?" he voiced with force while, grabbing Lee's white linen pao,[6] making the chair fall backwards with a loud bang. Lee pushed the rough hand away from his neck of his shirt, and uttered, "Gone, few days. Niece good woman. Not know other lady. Baby sick, now better," shaking his head. "We not know. Bishop Ben take them to Athens, maybe north. Baby better now. Okie dokie. We not know." At that, Anthony shoved the couple aside and like a bull stomped out the door and in one bound jumped on King's back heading now for Athens.

Lee hugged Acho to him. They comforted one another and began the new prayer they learned. "Our Father, which art in heaven."

———❧———

Anthony slowed down now that the ride was on the last few miles. He and his heart seemed to meet to sort out just how he got to where he was, just how things took a turn from the pride of Rome to disgust. How

---

[6] Chinese shirt

did a marriage end up with a mate dead, and he had not even had time to grieve like a loving husband—Right! Lying husband. A mess.

Maybe the Christian curses really are on all who helped in killing their so-called Savior. He also just couldn't shake how his close friend talked about his witness of this thing in Jerusalem and how the whole garrison looked on and spat on the man, and when he threw lots for the man's garment while his mother watched, the look on her face, and then the forgiveness. Was this the evil eye? Things went from bad to worse when the troops arrived back home. Maybe, no. He began to justify this drama. It served him right to have this all happen. The god's judgments are on me because I told a lie, and now the blessings are taken from me. With Margaret gone and now the child, the Roman gods doubled the rage. With the loss of two, they double the payment. The last half mile went by slowly now that his anger was subdued, and like a broken, wounded soldier-Minerva's free will-on his dark soul matching the eerie silence of the dark deserted streets at this midnight hour. He was trying to remember just when he and Margaret were here last to visit Kara and her three wee ones. Sad about the little boy with a speech problem, but he was a cute one, looking like her late husband. War costs more than just money and territory he thought as he dismounted from King and walked up the winding dirt pathway toward the lovely summer home.

He could see as he walked upon the porch that a small candle was still burning. Kara was up if she was true to her old habit. Many times, she has done some baking while everyone else was sleeping. Wiping his sandals as was his habit; he softly knocked and took a long slow breath in and then out.

"Now who could that be at this hour?" Kara wondered. Maybe Paula had returned with the baby and has had a change of heart and mind. Wiping her hands and picking up the candle, she headed toward the door. Upon opening the door, she could not believe her eyes. "Anthony, you, and where is that sister of mine, come now? Where have you hidden her? I know you both like surprises."

Anthony stepped inside and just motioned for Kara to head toward the kitchen, not wanting to wake up the children as it was now very late. He then, taking some very deep breaths, began to share the saga of the last several weeks of what he had endured and then the final event of what happened to Margaret. Kara just stared at him, hoping he was just joking, but no, she saw the serious frown lines and intense sadness of his own countenance. She just reached over, hugged, and held him, and in that moment, sadness was a joint companion. Wiping her eyes, she said that she was now a follower of the Christ and that she on her last visit had talked to Margaret. "I believe she too began to see that Minerva was not a true god to worship and was going to approach you about the matter. I guess she did not have the opportunity. Nor did she mention about what the doctor said about her heart."

"A child, Anthony? I know that Margaret could not have children, so what is this about a child?" He then explained without the full disclosure of his unfaithfulness but explained that Margaret thought he had saved the child from a dying couple. "She did not know that he was my own child. Then the illness, which had always plagued her, worsened from the smoke when our Domus caught fire." Anthony spoke on about his own view about Rome and about his friend watching while Jesus died in Jerusalem. Now he tells Kara that he is so heavy in heart and soul and disgusted with all the killing, especially of women and children. Kara knew that she was not as fluent a speaker as Bishop Ben, so she hoped for Anthony's sake that in the morning the Good News would be opened and shared. She hoped that now was the right time for Anthony and now would be the time for change in his life and heart—change from the false gods to the real and true God, the Messiah of the entire world.

Ahava—Donkey's Story

Paula headed quickly down the path, holding Drew closer to hush the few sounds that might again come from the baby. She glanced back behind her thankful that no one had seen her.

Paula creeping along the path without a problem and now on the road and heading for the shipping area was glad about the hidden knife. It gave her some comfort as it was beginning to get dark. During play with the children, Ahava stood alert. Her ears picked up subtle sounds of a child coming from behind the house. She left the children to head for the back of the house, passing the beautiful garden. No child. She kept on walking and went down the path to the gate and pushed it open, soon catching sight of Paula and the baby several yards away heading down the road toward the *wharf.*

Slowly, Ahava fell in step behind the wayward pair. Noticing her, Paula was startled but also glad to see her. Paula now walked along beside Ahava holding on to her ear for guidance, and soon Ahava's ear began to turn a dim glow. Finally, Ahava turned up a path which led to a small sheep-holding shed. She lifted the small gate closing and snorted, causing the sheep to move together in one corner while Ahava moved Paula and the baby back toward the east corner. Feeling with her hands, Paula found the straw bedding and knelt down on it. Inside her bundle, she remembered the candle, but without a fire, it was useless. One again she touched Ahava's ear as the full moon came out from some clouds, giving enough light for the moment. Paula's faith was beginning to increase. She remembered the story Peter told them one beautiful night about a barn scene, the angels singing in the sky when a baby boy born to a virgin in Bethlehem was laid in an animal trough. Mary called her son Jesus, but Peter was the one that convinced everyone that He was the Lamb of God who died on the cross for the sins of the world.

"Ahava, my heart is being pricked about leaving," she whispered, "and I don't understand this." The hard heart suddenly broke inside her, and she hugged the baby tightly to her breast, a baby that was at first just a child taken from a stranger's arms, a useful source of sympathy for a stranded mother, but now love for this babe filled her soul. Again, stroking Ahava and whispering, "Ahava, I don't understand. What is going on with my feelings?" But just then little Drew really let them know he was hungry. Suddenly, Paula's blouse grew wet when what was dried up and dead sprang to life and milk flowed. Her hand felt in disbelief then an overwhelming love flowed as Drew began to nurse.

Paula knew that Lesia and Bishop Ben recognized this real God, and their words grew alive now in her. "In the morning, Ahava, we will return, and I will join them in their love for Christ. What and where and which way I and Drew are to go, God will show us." Silent sleep fell on that little scene, so Ahava knelt for the nightly watch when the angel appeared, smiled, then left.

Kara and Anthony in the Kitchen

Morning came early for Lesia and Bishop Ben, both heading toward the kitchen where they found two sleeping adults. Looking at each other, they knew that from the dampened cloth by Kara's face, she must have gotten some very sad news.

Awakening almost simultaneously, Anthony was first to quickly stand, staring hard at Lesia and Bishop

Ben. Turning toward Kara, "You did not say that they were still here."

"Oh, Anthony, yes. I am sorry I wasn't clear, but they were planning on leaving this morning for the islands Cos and then on to Miletus."

Seeing this man her mind did a flashback to Rome, Lesia then broke the awkwardness by saying, "You, you, I believe you were the soldier that shoved me away from sure death by trampling when those runaway horses were fleeing from the fire in Rome." Anthony thought for a moment, "Yes, yes, but your hair, madam, was down." Smiling at that remembrance, Lesia just came forward and gave Anthony the hug he deserved, thankful for what he had done.

Kara turned toward the pantry came out with a dozen eggs and a slab of ham. She said, "while I am cooking you could go and search for Paula. She is confused and running from the truth is never the right way to go." So yawning, she tied on her apron as the three looked at each other. Lesia began, "Anthony, this young lady and the baby…"

But Anthony held up his hand to silence her. "Kara filled me in last night, but what you don't know is that my baby boy was kidnapped, and I am in pursuit of anyone who came from Rome with a child. He could be my son." At that he turned, Bishop Ben was right behind as Lesia fell in all heading for the front door. When a knock on the door came, silence fell over the group.

Kara came into the hall and passed all of them in their silence, looking at them as her hand reached to unlock and open the door. "PAULA!" echoed all of them in unison.

Stepping slowly in, Paula was at first unaware of Anthony. Lesia was right in her face taking the bundle of wiggling baby and hugging it lovingly. She then rushed out with him to the back of the house. "Oh no, my breakfast," exclaimed Kara, who took off toward the kitchen followed by Bishop Ben.

The hall now contained only two people, Anthony and Paula. Paula suddenly eye to eye with Anthony, without thinking reached down into her boot and brought out the knife. "You!" she voiced as she recognized who was before her. "You lowlife. What are you doing here? You were hard to my tears and to the time when a dead baby was hidden from me, no one came to my screams… You… YOUR LUST LIKE A BEAST…you…," with her hand still raise with the knife now swinging.

Bishop hearing the ruckus, rushed back toward the hall, and stepped in between Paula and Anthony. "Paula, get hold of yourself," he commanded as he took the knife out of her hand, then turning to Anthony, "My good man, you need to explain this and *right* now. How do you know Paula?"

Anthony first blurted out, "Please, let me see the baby. I need to see the child. Where did that lady take him?" looking around for Lesia.

Lesia returned with Drew just in time to Anthony's last statement. "Here, sir. He needed tending to, but you see, he is Paula's."

Anthony pulled back the blanket from around the loveliest child from heaven. Yes, yes, it was his baby. He twirled around with the child while the others stared. When the tears fell, everyone knew that even though a tough, trained soldier, he had a father's heart. "But this child cannot be yours," Lesia remarked again trying to take the child away from Anthony. Ben said, "Lesia, Paula took the baby and put his arms around her."

Anthony asked, "Please, I must speak to Paula alone if you would be so kind, and please, Lady Paula, will you hear me out?"

When everyone left Anthony and Paula alone, Anthony turned to Paula and said, "Paula, I know why you were running away from Rome. I read the report giving the account of your confrontation with Gaius, hitting him with a good size stone. Well, Gaius did not die. Paula, he did not die though you gave him quite a concussion. Thankfully, his skull was thick," smiling at the remembrance. "Gaius had me pay quite a price for you, but when I found that you were a lady, I continued to pay him so that he would not profit from you like the others."

"Remember the night of delivery? The midwife was paid handsomely to report that the child had died. I then paid the midwife again to take the baby to one of her family members who could nurse him for two months. After that, I took him home to my wife, Margaret. Margaret was ill and couldn't have children, so I told her that this baby was a gift from a Christian couple who were facing death at the hands of Nero. The fire, however, changed our plans. Because of Margaret's health, she was to take the child and set sail to Patras. She never knew that the baby was my own."

Paula gaped with astonishment at him, and on this, he knelt down before her on his knees, now she was standing frozen and unsure of what was happening, "Paula, he is our son. Paula, he is your baby boy." Paula promptly swooned, Anthony catching her just before she struck her head on the table.

Behind the kitchen door, a gasp could be heard as everyone had stayed to listen. Lesia entered the kitchen with her mouth open and tears flowing, hugging the child tightly, one big emotional muddle. "Oh my, Ben, we must have a wedding, mustn't we?" she sniffed.

"Hold on, child, remember they have to go to Rome first. Anthony needs to settle his military status, and Paula needs to check about her mother. Then it will be up to Paula." Breakfast was now early lunch among emotional adults with three children shaking their heads for lack of understanding. Ahava wished she was inside the house, but her ears were tingling, and she knew things were well in many ways. She picked up Andrews's sandal that had been dropped in the grass and placed it gently down at the door entrance. Then she heard its music and was soon turning in circles, letting out a bray that was heard by neighbors far and wide.

The children heard this, as well, and out the door they went running to witness a dancing donkey. Laughter sprang forth from the three lovely children who soon joined Ahava's antics with actions of their own.

Again, Bishop Ben can share this experience of the Good News. The Gospel message of the love of Jesus is for everyone: for boys and girls, as well as for adults.

No one left that day. Paula and Anthony accepted their destiny along with their newfound faith, meaning they now rejected the Roman gods. Ben let them know that in Berea he had met a man called Paul, who had stayed there for three months building a new church. Part of Ben's job was to deliver a letter to those who loved the new faith here in Greece. In it Paul explained how he had found Jesus. He told them, "I am not ashamed of the gospel, because it is the power of God for the salvation of everyone who believes: first for the Jew, then for the Gentile. For in the gospel righteousness from God is revealed, righteousness that is by faith from first to last, just as it is written: 'The righteous will live by faith.'"

Captain DeStefano

The captain barked orders as the ship was slowly being docked in Athenian waters in the early morning light. The storm had damaged one sail, so until the repair is completed, everyone is to have shore leave. "Yar better not shame me name or me ship because when we set sail and the northeast wind sprays me face with the great sea, ye will be whipped to an inch of your worthless skull."

The captain gathers up grapes, cheese, and wine, which came from Joppa. He knows that Kara will love these items and begins to consider what to gather for the children. "Apples, sweet pears, and yes, the she cat and her two kittens. Yes, Isidora, Tomas, and Zita Maria[7] will love them." The cats had similar markings to an earlier bunch he had seen months ago. "There is nothing like cats to carry on their breed on water or land," he mused.

Slowly proceeding down several lanes to his daughter-in-law's home, he shuffled his bundles between his shoulders and his strong back. Stepping upon the small stone porch, he noticed a sandal by the door. He picked it up while setting down his other heavy packs. Then he gave a hearty, hearty knock!

Kara hurried to the door. "Captain, what?" And while her question went unanswered, the three children jumped into their grandpa's arms. "Okay, okay, enough. You must see what I have for ye, Tommy, come here." He went back out onto the porch and retrieved the small basket, which was meow, meow, meowing. This meowing gave away the secret gift. Captain also laid the sandal down in the entrance where Lesia saw it.

"Oh, the sandal Paula thought had gotten lost back at the sheep holding pen at the wharf," Lesia cried. Picking it up, she hurriedly left toward her own room

---

[7] Zita little girl

for a moment of privacy. "Oh, Andrew, this is part of you. How beautiful are your feet that served the faith message for God?" She embraced the sandal and for a moment, she pretended Andrew was laughing and holding her again. She could remember his wonderful smile, and though his hands were fishermen's rough, sea-worn hands, they always were soft and gentle to her face.

Kara introduced her father-in-law and declared that he was just the best man in the world. She had been proud to have loved his son. He exuded a powerful presence, the occupation of captain fitting him perfectly. Anthony knew that fate once again was at hand in his life. He knew that this captain would play a role.

Captain DeStefano—Now is in the decisions concerning Anthony and Paula for passage back to Rome. Anthony hugging Paula said, as soon as we get home we will start looking for your mother, I promise as his thoughts went to his father. Anthony's father has many connections that could be helpful. He knew of several cells of Christians who had not been gathered up by the guards, delayed because of the fire and the unrest among the peasants.

Paula was trying to digest mentally and physically all that just happened to her in a twenty-four-hour period. A mother, she was the baby's real, honest-to-goodness, true mother. She was excited and felt somewhat redeemed from the hardship Anthony had put her through. He really deserved death, but Jesus said forgive others and He will forgive you. There is no better time than now to put in place obedience to God's word, like Peter said one night in the Catacombs as he broke into singing, "Hear O Israel, the Lord God is ONE God, for we did not follow devised myths. We have been eyewitness of his majesty. The Father said, 'This is my beloved Son.' Prepare your minds, discipline yourselves, set all your hope on the grace that Jesus Christ will bring you. Like obedient children, do not be conformed to the desires that you formerly had in ignorance. Serve a Holy God."

"Now should I be blessed also with a believing husband?" "God," she whispered, "come into my heart and help me be the best mother I can be to this child, and let love bloom between Anthony and me."

Lesia was in a struggle herself. She had promised the elderly couple that she would give Andrew's sandals to someone. Should it be this child? Paula when approached refused to take them, stating, "These sandals are special, Lesia, and I feel that Andrew would agree. They are to be yours for now," hugging her. They both laughed, and now they both recognized that the sandal on Drew's foot had the healing power in it.

Meanwhile, the men had their heads together, and Captain Jack had the right answers. "I will take Bishop Ben and Lesia and that animal up to Cos. Ah, excellent wine, wheat, silk, and ointment for healings was picked up on my last visit if I recall right, so I will profit from the small sail north. No need for you to worry about any expenses. Then I will come back for Anthony and Paula and that blessed baby boy. I must not tarry longer as I already took two days instead of one for fixing my torn sail. So, it's off in the morning with all of ye. For now, I want to go back down to the ship and get it ready for the launch. See that ye are there bright and early.

On that he hugged all the children more than once and his daughter-in-law, reminding her that his son made a good choice when he asked for her hand. "Ye are the darling that blesses me soul and the children. Until I see you again, I bid you God's blessing, and may the wind be me kind companion.

Cos[8]

The large plane tree in the center of town is called "the tree of Hippocrates" to this day. Cos was now commercial and industrial, in addition to being one of the Jewish centers in the Aegean. Lesia and Bishop Ben found themselves standing in the center of town, looking at and touching the famous tree[9].

Finally, they asked where they could find some place to shelter them and a donkey for the night. People mentioned that Yolie's relative Huldah Heimberger rebuilt such a place and a pen for animals. This will work out fine for Ahava so they headed down toward the outside of the little town.

The building was built with large and colorful stones, formerly used as a good old tavern. Huldah changed it into a way station for travelers that also provided meals. "We need to get something to eat," Lesia mentioned, "and after we get settled, we could come back down to the wharf and check on the smaller fishing vessels for hire."

Knocking on the big, old rustic door, Ben was greeted by a sweet old granny-type lady.

---

[8] Cos was the birthplace of Hippocrates (the father of Medicine).

[9] The plane tree in the center of town is called "the tree of Hippocrates" to this day. It was commercial and industrial, in addition to being one of the Jewish centers in the Aegean. https//en.wikipedia.org/wiki/Tree_of_Hippocrates.

"Welcome, travelers. Come in, come in." After a few introductions, exchanging information: names, port of departure, traveling itinerary, and other idle chatter. Huldah shared, "In the back of my establishment, I have started a dorm for homeless children." At that she rang a bell and they all came running: Alma, Eunice, Priscilla, Junia, Phoebe, Felicitas, Blandina, Michael, John, and Ted. They are my cleaning and yard maintenance crew, helping one another. Yes, on the left side of the stairs of this enlarged hall is the dining area. So, I hope you both are hungry."

"Hungry! We are starved," expressed the two together.

Huldah said, "John, you take Bishop Ben to the boy's area. Also show him around so that he can freshen up."

"Now my dear, let me take you back to the eating area." Huldah wanted to impress Lesia, recognizing a generous and kind woman who could be a big help to her. Wow, Lesia was impressed. They had set up a very nice area for extended tables and smaller ones for one or two. Huldah had made colorful covers for each table, and flowers decorated the room on the counters and tables. She had used statutes in the corners for height and had placed a Roman fountain in the middle. Lesia was quite surprised and pleased with the atmosphere. It was so delightful and inviting.

Huldah then began to explain to Lesia, "Unbelievable fate stepped into my life one day. Just when I began to despair because I couldn't keep up with all the work: cooking, cleaning, and washing. I had begun taking care of lost or abandoned children of all ages, even some infants, adding them as a part of my family. I prayed to the God above, and one night a tired traveler seeking just a bed for the night came into my life. He asked me where my kitchen was located, calling me an honest, good woman, and on that note, was blushing. We were all astonished the next morning when the bell rang, and we were presented with a lavish breakfast."

"Of course, he began to win the hearts of the children, and soon one night had turned into a year. I myself have fallen in love with such a kind and caring individual." For a second, the aroma coming from the kitchen seemed familiar to Lesia, but no jogging of her memory. It just must be a similar dish that Mara used to cook for them in Jerusalem.

"Come, you will meet him later. For now, you need to go to your room. Priscilla will show you where to refresh yourself. Just listen for the bell to ring, then come back down here to, of course, the largest of all our rooms."

Priscilla was a sweet young child and very talkative, chattering that she enjoyed when visitors would come. They liked to hear about where travelers lived or where they have traveled. Although some were nice, others were not. They arrived at the second floor and turned down the hallway to the right. Going to the second door, Pricilla opened the door to a nice clean room with comforters covering two individual cots, everything neat and orderly. Glad you said you wouldn't mind sharing this room with me. Priscilla then turned toward a curtain, covering an area where a large, Greek decorated water basin and water pitcher sat. Small towels were on a makeshift shelf, along with Greek oils and soaps. Lesia smiling said, "No way" Priscilla as Priscilla pulled back the curtain. "Yes, and make sure you use my special cream, even a girl with freckles needs it."

Ahh. Lesia had begun to miss the richness she had in Herodias's household, artisan bathing and several oils from the very heart of the Roman wares. She also missed sunbathing in secret on hidden areas on roof tops, but alas, she was here now, and looking at her hands, neglect was written all over them.

A smaller area showed more privacy, containing a large pot with a secured lid. Priscilla excused herself and went bouncing out the door, loudly saying as she was leaving, "We are also taking care of your donkey. He is a funny one. He pulled off the ribbon from Alma Delores's hair. Don't worry, he didn't hurt anyone but did like the chase we gave him."

The weather today had been hotter than usual, so the cool water and refreshing ointment soothing her aching muscles felt like the rich palace of Caesar. Lesia changed her blouse and skirt and lay down for a few minutes. Then she heard the bell. Rising, she brushed her hair and smiled, thinking about Ahava taking the child's ribbon from her hair. Ahava was doing different things again, and on that note, she turned and headed down the stairs passing a main room and then headed toward the large kitchen and dining area.

Bishop was already there and was in conversation with the children. He had chosen the larger table, so it looked like they would all share it. Eunice was now coming from the kitchen with two baskets of rolls, as well as wheat and pumpernickel bread. Huldah was seating several older adult travelers and chatting away. Lesia watched her gesture with her hands just like a good Italian servant back in Rome. Lesia looked around as Alma, Eunice, Priscilla, Junia, Phoebe,

Felicitas, Blandina, Michael, and John were taking their places. Bishop Ben was enjoying the ritual hellos and have you washed your hands, playing a good father figure. "Wait. I think Ted is missing," Lesia commented. Lesia sat at the end of the table with her back toward the kitchen door. She wanted to view all the children as her thoughts turned to Drew: would he grow up and be as chatty as these orphans? "Yes, Ted is missing. Phoebe, have you seen Ted?"

"Yes, ma'am. He was talking to the donkey and rubbing his ears and laughing and acting like he and that animal were talking. Ma'am, I guess he didn't hear the bell, so I will go get him."

"No, you sit right here. I will go and consider the matter. Ben save some food for me. I will be back after I see what is going on. I know that Ahava acts different, so maybe another God-sky spell is working."

Tracing all the way through the halls and going to the front door, Lesia didn't know yet that there was a shortcut, but she would in due time. She headed toward the end of the path and turned left to go toward the back of the big inn. Whew, better slow down as she was walking fast and felt her forehead getting sweaty. "Ted," she began to call, but no answer. "Ted, it is time to eat," she yoo-hooed. But the only answer she got was Ahava braying and returning to her bucket of oats. No Ted. She looked around some more, as well as inside the shed, but no child.

Well, he must have gone in, but he didn't pass me, she thought. So, she retraced her steps and on the way in escorted two more traveling people toward the dining hall. "Yes, Huldah was right. This is a lot of work. I only took care of Kara's three," she said, smiling at that memory.

Yes, Ted was there, and all had begun the joy of eating an enormous lunch. No one was interested in her heavy breathing, a result of her small jog from the shed. Anyway, she too settled herself, and by then the water and juice were in place. She poured a glass of water, feeling its coolness, and the coolness of the dining room was also a blessing in the noontime heat. Ben was placing a big piece of fried chicken on his plate with side helpings of turnip greens and mashed potatoes with goat's milk and cheese whipped in and a dash of curry. Then there were the fish dishes arranged in rows of fried to poached and steamed on lovely long leaves of special Greek greens. Rice tossed with roasted nuts alongside was also available, not to mention grapes, pears, and apples, which she knew came from the ship's larder of Captain DeStefano.

She too got lost in the joy of eating as she finally realized how hungry she really was. She couldn't remember when she ate last. The conversation was not dull as each child seemed to have a tale about what the others did. Yes, the children all seemed to be happy here and yet underneath each one had a horrid tale.

Huldah finally came in from the kitchen, and after seeing that all in the big hall were satisfied, she came over to Lesia and Ben's table. Huldah smiled and said, "My new cook, as I mentioned earlier, was a lonely and sick traveler. He was going back to his homeland to die. But I said, 'Oh, no you don't,' not with me being a good caregiver, and in no time, I had him better and full of life. I also fell in love with this man. He is so sweet and kind, and he can cook like an angel. Who would want anything more than that?" Lesia was laughing then Huldah said, "Okie dokie," and Lesia choked on her water.

"What did you just say, Huldah?"

"Oh, just a slang word. Hee, hee, my cook says it all the time. Lesia, why the strange look on your face? Are you all right? Did you choke on too much water?"

Lesia stood up and dashed toward the kitchen door and swung it open. Her eyes could not believe what she saw. Older and grayer, ponytail draped over slumped shoulders, but it was the best sight she could imagine—her father.

She greeted him while he was in the middle of attending to his pots and pans. It was always the first thing he did after cooking even before resting. At the sound of Lesia's voice, he turned sharply. This time it was Mara Chin who fainted away.

"Huldah, help, I killed him. I should not have surprised him," she said, now holding his head in her lap. Nurse Huldah stepped into action and soon with the help of her salts, Mara was coming around. His eyes looked up into a face he thought he would never see or touch again. Lesia started blubbering and soon two people were united once again because neither distance nor time can erase human connections of souls.

"Well, daughter, okie dokie. I okay now. Let's get tea going. Tea cure nerves."

"Yes, Father, always."

The next few weeks were wonderful. Arrangements were made with Bishop Ben to marry the couple, and Lesia gave her blessing repeatedly. "I want you happy, Father. Since I now know that my mother would never have given me away if my real father had been alive, you are the only father I know. And you will always be my father." On that note, Mara Chin felt good inside. They began to realize that the good God above (sky) had His hand on them both.

After Bishop Ben does the honors, he wants to head north toward Miletus and then go over to the new church in Ephesus. He had heard that the Ephesus church has some prison letters from Paul brought to them by Tychicus and he was eager to hear more of Paul's doctrine.

One morning, Lesia went out to tend to Ahava when the donkey brought her the ribbon. "What, here you are acting different again. I guess you want me to return this to Alma Delores even though it was you that yanked it from her hair. That was not a very nice donkey. Now I will have to wash and press it, so I guess I will get to it. You are like a small puppy always getting into trouble." Little did she know that this was another small mission.

The children were listening to Bishop Ben expounding religious teaching from information he had learned. Lesia came from her room carrying the blue-ribbon ready for Alma's hair—the ribbon no worse for wear. "Alma, come here dear," Lesia called. She had Alma sit down in front of her so she could place the ribbon around the hair. Lifting the heavy locks, she stopped a moment, noticing that the one side of Alma's face had been burned. "Is that why she covers her hair more to that side?" Lesia wondered. "How did this happen, and why haven't I noticed it before now?" Clearing her thoughts, she decided to engage Alma into conversation. "You are a beautiful young lady. I guess you look like your mother."

"Yes, but a tragedy changed all of our lives," Alma sadly said. "Oh, I am so sorry. If you want to tell me or talk to me later, you may come to me at any time." On that Alma got a sweet, big hug and smiled as the bow was tied above her head. She set her hair in motion, swinging it from side to side. Then it happened. Alma pulled more hair over to her right side, probably not realizing what she was doing. Lesia, now more alert to God-sky's, just shook her head. *Ahava, you old donkey, you are different, but a God blessing. Don't worry, old donkey, I shall see what we can do for this child*, Lesia thinks to herself.

Lesia decided to talk to Huldah about this matter and see what else she could find out about Alma. Huldah was busy changing beds in the big dorm sleeping room for the girls as Lesia approached her. "Here let me help you," and soon handmade sheets were off and clean were on. "Huldah, how did you get Alma? She sure loved getting her ribbon back from Ahava."

"Hmm…let me see. I believe she came from Rome where they had a six-day fire."

"What? So, you have had her just a short while."

"Yes, the ship brought in several people, but when it left, no one came forward to claim this child. I just happened to be there, getting some wares for my inn and noticed her sobbing beside her little bundle that the captain gave her. Well, me mother's blessing, that child was coming with me, so now, Missy, she is a lovely addition to our group, won't you agree? Hand me that pillow, thank you," and with a slap of the hands, the pillow was fluffed and in place.

Silently, Lesia left the room with Huldah. Thinking back on the conversation, she had thought that Alma was truly an orphaned child, but on second thought recognized that something was not right. The burn was an old one, almost fading in some spots. Yes, Lesia concluded, Alma was afraid of something that happened earlier in her life where she felt she was to blame or ashamed, or maybe it was just an unfortunate accidental fire. Lesia didn't get much sleep because of the concern for Alma, knowing from the signal of the ribbon that she and Ahava were to do something for this lovely child. Rome? What if her mother is still alive? Turning more than once on her little cot, she finally fell asleep.

Hearing the early bell, Lesia knew she must rise and go help her father with breakfast. Opportunity to intercede with Alma would come when Alma asked to help feed Ahava and do some yard chores. It was good idea that at breakfast the children were assigned chores or could ask for tasks they wanted to do. *If I ever would run an orphanage, I certainly would want to steal many of Huldah's ideas*, Lesia thought. This was the first time Lesia had ever contemplated about her future.

The chores were finished, and it was quiet as they sat around the fire in a large kettle cauldron. Summer will be giving way to fall so many decisions had to be made and soon. The final decision was determined that if Alma Delores was from Rome, she could be sent back to Athens to Kara, who could connect her with Paula and Anthony. They would either become her godparents or, with Anthony's connection, would look for any surviving relatives. Lesia was to be the one to talk to Alma about these plans for her future.

Lesia came upon Alma making a sign in the small sand area beside the back garden gate and the rose bushes. "Well, what do we have here?" asked Lesia, walking forward to glance over the child's shoulder. "A fish drawing?"

Alma looked up and started to rub out the picture, acting like she was caught doing something wrong. "No, Alma," Lesia said as she knelt and began to draw her fish symbol in the sand. "Who showed you this? Where did you see it?"

"My mother drew this one day and told me it was to be our secret. Then sometimes she would go to secret meetings and leave my brother and me at home. Miss Lesia, I lied to everyone about how my face was burned. It didn't get burned in the fire in Rome. It really happened one day when Mom was gone, and I got too close to the burn pit and caught my hair on fire. I'm sorry I lied, but I didn't want to admit the truth and seem bad in your eyes.

"I was ashamed because my family never talked about it even to this day. The night of the Rome's fire, I and my brother ran out of the house. Somewhere in the madness of it, I got lost and an older man and woman grabbed me and carried me along with their family. I yelled several times for my brother, but he was not found in the crowd, and when that family boarded the ship, the mother just took my hand against my will. All I had was a small bundle in my hand. The woman took my bundle and later got off at one of the islands without telling me. I was left alone on the ship, totally lost, so I hid till a one-eyed cat came and slept by my side in the dark of the night. I kept petting him, and soon I fell fast asleep.

"Later, some of the ship's men carried me up to the captain, and they talked about me. I was so afraid that they were going to throw me overboard. I guess I started to cry. An old man pulled out his harmonica and started playing, trying to make me stop crying. He was trying to get me to laugh instead. He told the captain he would take care of me until we reached Cos. When we got here, Miss Huldah was at the dock. I saw her talking to the captain for a long time. Soon I was walking by her side and coming to the Tavern Inn. I love it here, but my brother and my mother could be still alive. Maybe, Miss Lesia."

At that note, tears began flowing, "Maybe, but I heard someone say that Nero started the fire by using the Christians and what if my mother was one of his victims, then I really would be an orphan. Please don't be angry at me. I am so scared."

At that Lesia assumed her hugging mode, reassuring this child that the God who sees everything also sees her and her problem. "We have a plan." Lesia then explained the details. "When you get to Kara's home in Athens, you will love her and her three children.

Tommy (Tomas) who had a speech problem was touched by God, and we are sure that God will work out His plan for your life, as well. Now, let's go in and clean up and get ready to let everyone know the rest of the story." Hand in hand, they walked silently back around the inn toward the entrance where Huldah was again greeting some new strangers for lunch.

Friday evening was soon approaching, so Mara Chin had made some special dessert to go along with the Sabbath meal. Huldah placed her little white lace scarf on her neatly plaited hair and said as she lit the candle, "Blessed are you, Lord, our God, King of the Universe who has sanctified us by His command to us to kindle the Sabbath light." Then she blessed the bread, "Blessed are you, Lord, our God, King of the universe who brings forth bread from the earth." We laughed and talked then the Spirit of the Lord quickened Bishop Ben's heart to share what he had learned from Paul, who was called at one-time Saul. The children began to quiet down and Mara Chin stopped cleaning the kitchen. As the gospel was opened in his physical ears, his spiritual ears became quickened, as well. He recognized that God had given back his health. "Ears hear, love. God love me. Heart funny inside. Want God too, okie dokie."

Excitedly, Bishop Ben began with Paul's testimony, how he, a man who studied at the feet of Gamaliel and trained for the law, came to believe in Jesus Christ. Paul's background made him a prominent man in his culture. He was the son of a Pharisee of Roman citizenship, born in the city of Tarsus, located at the northeast corner of the Mediterranean Sea. Bishop Ben talked of Saul's heart. At first Paul thought he was doing right in not accepting these Christians since he was a Jew and the Jews believed in God only, not Jesus Christ. He thought he was pleasing God through his persecutions.

Pricilla exclaimed, "Oh my, Uncle Ben, that's horrible what he did to Stephen, holding his coat and maybe even throwing a stone himself." The rest of the children agreed.

"Go on, Uncle Ben," said Ted. Then Bishop Ben explained how God blinded Saul on the road to Damascus and told him that he was to go to the house of Ananias near Straight Street in Damascus. "Saul was blind for three days in which he said he searched his very soul. Ananias, the prophet, ministered to Saul and opened the door of Jesus Christ to him. He heard about how a virgin would bring forth a male child who would be called Emmanuel, God with us. Saul then remarked that when he was struck down on the Damascus road, a voice identified himself as Jesus whom he had persecuted. From that point, Saul became Paul and fervently preached the Faith. Soon he was rejected by the Jews then God called him to go preach to the Gentiles.

"Paul said he received the work of Jesus Christ on the cross by faith, and we who are Jews, physically or spiritually, have a choice. We also by faith must believe. This man, Jesus Christ, the Son of God, is the one we have been waiting for. As a Gentile, you have to choose to be grafted into the Covenant of Abraham."

Little Alma spoke up and said, "My mother got Jesus Christ into her heart. I want that, too." Before the night was over, all the children came to believe in the Jewish man call Jesus, and by faith accepted Him into their hearts. Mara Chin wiped away tears along with Lesia and Huldah. Salvation really had come to the little Tavern Inn in the small island of Cos.

Priscilla was still teary-eyed at bedtime. Lesia went over to her, hugged her, and explained that what she was feeling was the presence of the Holy Spirit. With that Lesia said, "Ted and you are the oldest ones here and soon will be at the marrying age. You must choose a mate that loves Jesus now that you have him in your heart." Inside, Lesia choked back a tear herself, thinking of Andrew, his smile and his laugh, and how one time he went on and on and on about Jesus. Priscilla's laughter startled Lesia back to reality as Priscilla's exclaimed, "What? Who will love a redhead with lots of freckles? Anyway, Huldah will be needing help, and I want to stay here and help her. She has become my second mom and has promised to teach me the art of weaving. Some good rugs and blankets will help the Inn, and maybe sold to earn some money for us."

"Oh, that would be great, and if I stay over to winter here, I too will learn with you as I can thread a needle now in the dark," she said, smiling as she moved to her little cot. She bent down and pulled out the small box, which held some of her personal things. She removed

Andrew's sandals and holding them she smelled them again that fresh sweet rose odor that still lingered on them. Turning to Priscilla, she remarked, "I'll be back. You go ahead to bed. I need to say good night to Ted and Alma."

Heading down the hall, Lesia went toward the boy's quarters, knocking gently on the door. "Ted, Michael. Are you boys still awake?"

Ted opened the door. "Miss Lesia, are things okay?"

"Yes, yes, Ted. I wanted to give you Andrew's left sandal. Please sleep with it tonight. Would you do that for me?" Puzzled, an awkward, growing boy reached for the sandal and closed the door.

Michael was asleep, thank goodness, thought Ted as he quickly entered his side of the bed and placed the sandal beside his leg. *Sleeping with a shoe. What odd things women think up for children to do*, thought Ted as he slowly succumbed to sleep.

During the night, Ted remembered some of his childhood with his stepmother, how his stepmother would take away his musical flutes. "You can't sit around with notes in yar head when thar is work to be done. Now out with ye to the barn, and not one drop of milk do ye lose. Ya hear me? Now, get!" Then the musical notes from flutes and lyres floated into the scene along with the brief image of a bull and a matador. The music soothed his soul and healed his mind of verbal abuse received in earlier years.

Upon rising early, the next morning, Ted went down on his knees beside the bed. Pulling out a small box, he brushed off the dust and then slowly took off the lid. The flute that he had packed along with a few other things when he ran away from the farm was still there. He picked it up and, with a gift of a musical ear, began playing one of the tunes he had heard during the night: the same tunes that Andrew had heard on the night the Lord called to him to preach the Good News. Ted now had a calling on his life, a call to go to Spain, but for now his soul was as free as the music which floated throughout the bedroom.

Michael, rising upon one arm, said, "Wow, that was awesome. I didn't know you could do that. May I try to blow it?"

"Yes, of course," and Ted handed the flute to the wide-eyed, messy-haired boy.

After a few tries, Michael stopped playing and handed the flute back to Ted. "No, I am not musical," and laughter began their day.

Meanwhile after Lesia left Ted's room, she proceeded to check on Alma. Quietly tiptoeing into her room, she slipped the right sandal in beside the sleeping child. "Oh, Andrew. You and God are still doing His work. Yes, a miracle will happen, and a child's face will be restored." Love will do it. Love that will come through on a sandal. The amazing, un-measureable love from the Creator of all the handiwork will kiss this child.

Bishop Ben came into the dining area with some exciting news that he had gotten down at the harbor when going to get the latest talk and check on any ships that would be suitable to go forward with the plan to send Alma Delores back to Athens. They were afraid that the voyage to Rome would be too long for an unchaperoned child. He exclaimed, "What luck. A Spanish sailing ship, the *Silver Eagle*, is in the harbor. I've brought Captain Miguel Stalladora here to meet everyone. He will be sailing to Athens within the week." Huldah, of course, was now seating Miguel at a small table. Exciting chatter erupted with the thought that just maybe Alma Delores would now get to Rome if passage was possible with this captain. *We must check him out*, thought Bishop Ben. *We do not want Alma Delores to be a victim ever again.*

Breakfast was excellent as usual, and Miguel turned out to be friendly and trustworthy. He began to explain his current journey. He told the group that he was in the process of scouting out opportunities for the Queen, trying to find more trading options in various ports and with the small islands in the Mediterranean Sea. He had already visited Alexandria, Egypt, and Joppa. Now after leaving Cos, he planned to sail to Miletus, then back down to Athens.

Miguel had brought some wares with hoping to exchange or sell the items at each port of call. In fact, he had left a large box of things in the hall beside the entrance door. The box contained expensive pottery and eloquent clothing he had picked up in Joppa, hoping to contact some purchasers here in Cos.

Bishop Ben wanted to find out Miguel's religious thoughts, but each time he was about to approach this subject, someone would ask Miguel about Spain. "What is in your merchant ship?" asked Ted.

"We picked up a nice load of furniture and cheese."
"Have you been to Rome?"

"What is Spain like?"

"Did you ever see Nero?" Interruptions now coming from three others.

"So many questions. Well, let me start with Rome. Merchants come to us. We serve as a granary for the Roman market. We also export gold, wool, olive oil, and wine. My father had his own merchant ships with a large export business between Spain and Rome.

Now about my city. I live in Barcelona on the eastern coast of Spain. It is a beautiful, dynamic city with an excellent harbor, good climate and calm seas. When I am home from the sea, I enjoy the challenge of catching and eating from the great varieties of fresh and salt water fish. I would not want to live anywhere else.

"Ah, Nero, he is a strange one. Father saw him, but I did not want to because of the talk about how pompous he was. My beautiful queen is enough for me. But I would hear the talk when down at the Roman wharf. It was quite explosive, and of course, my good friend would let me know just what he felt. There was always a lot of the talk about Christians. Nero did not think kindly of you, right?"

"I also heard talk while in Joppa. There were words about things that happened in Jerusalem. I am not sure about your God, but I do know that when in a middle of a terrible storm on the sea, all of us often call out for mercy."

Miguel inwardly trembled as he thought of his experience several months ago with a man called Paul. Bishop Ben and the others didn't realize how close to a nerve they struck as God was discussed. Even saying the name of God is enough to cause Miguel to cringe.

Miguel's ship had sailed out of Cyprus on its journey to Joppa. Paul and his friend called Luke boarded there and asked just where he was planning to stop. They mentioned that they wanted to go to Spain and then later to Rome. He told them his was the ship to take as he had a full load and needed to head home. They seem very pleased with this news and said they would return shortly.

Miguel barked orders for his men to hurry the loading process then he double-checked his list. Once the ship was fully ladened, an exceptionally heavy load this time, he glanced toward the sky and pondered the thought, *Please, no storms.*

Looking at Paul, he wondered what this man's ailment might be to have a doctor traveling with him. Luke remarked that they had just come from

Jerusalem, ministering to the poor with goods from Macedonia and Achaia. They did not look worse from their worrisome travel, so Miguel felt he did not have to coddle two strangers, especially one a Jew. He went below, checking to see where they might be given some reasonable comfort. He decided to let them have a small room beside his own cabin.

"Cast off. Drop the spring lines," he ordered. He was surprised when the ship caught a perfect breeze, making him able to slowly ease her out toward the open sea. There was nothing like a cool night with a full moon shining to calm the sailors' fears, even soothing the captain. They all could gaze at the stars. Some even remarked about how they were able see clearly even without the use of the eyeglass. Best of all, the captain allowed a small bit of port to be shared. While in this relaxed mood, one of Miguel's older sailors began to blow a small tune upon his instrument.

Paul and Luke also joined the men on deck, and Miguel could see that they were discussing their Jerusalem pursuits. Turning the ship's wheel over to his second in command, he joined them. "You two are not first timers on ships," he commented, and this was the beginning of some of the stories he heard about their travels. "Running from a mob of people wanting to kill you must have taken super strength, right?"

"Wrong," said Paul, and then he began telling about meeting Jesus on the road to Damascus. He shared how he came to believe in Him, the only Son of the Highest God. He explained how the Ephesians had a hard time hearing about a real God versus the Roman goddess Diana and the Greek goddess Artemis. These were the goddesses noted for hunting, the moon, and fertility, but the Highest God is the creator of all.

Miguel felt uncomfortable, so he excused himself and went back toward the wheel. During the rest of the night with just a few sailors on upper deck, he began to think about himself and his beliefs. To Miguel, it sounded like a far-fetched story, yet he remembered that some of his neighbors had been Jewish. They keep the laws and even wanted him to become Jewish. He knew that their God kept His people for forty years in the desert, feeding them daily manna, then brought them out to a new land flowing with milk and honey. Just then the breeze began to increase, so he became engrossed in watching the sails.

"Lower the backs ones down some," commanded Miguel. Then just the sky was about to dump from the open heavens, it grew calm again. He couldn't understand why he was showing the jitters. Sailing with his uncle since he was a little lad, he now was the owner of the Silver Eagle. His father had built quite a good, rich business, owning part of the wharf and storage buildings and boat sheds. Miguel had inherited the Silver Eagle as well as the Flying Falcon, along with an abundant portion of grain, wine, olive oil, and gold from his father. Never wanting to marry even though the maids were always willing, he remembered a time when he came close. There was one Jewish girl he really wanted to be with, but she too began believing this God thing. She and her parents tried to convert him to their laws and customs, and when he rebelled, one night she slapped his face so hard his jaw ached for days. Still he was almost ready to capitulate when Rita came into the picture. Rita and her togas and Rome spas. Soon the bell rang for changing the watch, and Miguel was brought back to his duties and responsibilities as captain. Louis took over the wheel, allowing Miguel to go below to the storage area where he rechecked and retied bundles to make sure things were still snug and tight. He found Samuel in the corner not looking very well. "Blazes, man, what happened?" Samuel, having had too much grog, had fallen into a drunken sleep, and an akhbar had taken a piece out of his leg. He helped Samuel toward the upper deck where several other men began to cut away the pants and throw the bloody pieces overboard.

"You drunken pig," said one. "Serves ye right to steal away and take more than your share. Shut up, or when I can, I will put your mouth behind ye ears." Then Luke appeared with Paul. Miguel turned to begin an explanation, but Paul was turning toward Luke, and Luke was already down on his knees looking at the gash.

"Sorry, old man," said Luke, "but it will have to be washed and the seawater is salty so this is going to hurt. Bite on this belt." Luke then told Miguel his stitches were a few, but the gash was deeper than he liked. However, if the fever didn't come upon him, he thought Samuel could return to his post shortly.

Then Paul began again to tell about his conversion experience. "I was stubborn and bullheaded about God's, son Jesus, but soon found out that Jesus truly is the Son of God." Again, Miguel excused himself and went to the farthest part of the ship. However, once again Paul's words had hit a nerve inside Miguel. "What is he?" Miguel pondered. He is educated in several languages, and it sounds like he came from some money and good, upper-class people. A Jew having love and compassion toward Gentiles. Is he real? Why am I letting this man get under my skin?"

Miguel decided that in the future he must remember not to let Paul on board again no matter what. He could really understand now how Paul could preach way into the wee hours of the night. "Possessed, that is what he is. He sings and talks Hebrew way into the night, and of course, he is just a door away from my hearing." Miguel finally pulled the small pillow around both of his ears.

For two more days, Miguel survived the agony. His crew were continuously sitting at the man's feet, hanging onto all his words and damn with the sails. "Back to work," shouted Miguel. "Ye think ye are on vacation or holiday?" Then looking at Paul, shaking his head and sighing under his breath, "Asquear! So, innocent? No way. He made us one day later by bewitching the men, and we missed a good headwind. Now what else might happen?" churned through Miguel's mind.

"Good morning, Captain," said Samuel, "and by the way, Captain, if you have never seen or heard about healings, just feast those peepers of yars on my calf. You better believe it. The fever went and the leg turned from black to brown, just like it had never been chewed on. Captain, where are you going? The wheel, sir?"

"Let your God take the wheel!" fumed Miguel. Hurrying now to talk to Luke, he found him on the lower deck praying and writing. He then slowly turned and thought, *Oh my, am I crazy, leaving Samuel at the wheel.* If feet had wings, Miguel made it appear so as he sprinted double-time up the stairs and back to Samuel.

"Why, Captain, whar's the trust on me," mutters old Samuel. "You didn't know it was in me, did you now?" No, he didn't know. Why had this been overlooked? Many times, a good backup is a gift of gold.

"Miguel, Miguel," Bishop Ben called louder and louder. "Are you all right?"

"Oh, pardon sir. I must have dozed off. Lack of sleep, I suppose, so please forgive."

"Now we can fix that. You shall stay the night here if Huldah agrees," motioning with his hand to her to come over to the table. "Huldah, is it all right for the captain to stay here at the inn today. It seems that he has had a very long night."

"Yes, yes, sir. It will be our pleasure," and she motioned him to follow her as she continued her chatter. "He can have Mara Chin's excellent breakfast and then stay in the extra room. On and on she prattled.

As Miguel settled in his room, his thoughts turned once again to Paul. Getting away from Paul had been a great relief, but then Paul did an unexpected thing. He had hugged Miguel and gave him an apron, telling him that the apron would bless him. By this time, most of the crew had accepted Christ and had even thrown their idols overboard into the sea. Paul told Miguel that he would be praying for him so that he too would become a believer, marry, and become prosperous as his soul prospered.

A believer? No way! thought Miguel. As soon as the ship anchored in Rome, he planned to forget about Paul. The talk as he left Rome was all about the Christians this and Christians that, and Nero was having a field day with them. He determined that to die so young was not going to happen to him, so throwing the apron over his bed, he gave it no more thought. Till tonight!

Bishop Ben thought to himself that there was more here than met the eye. When God's name was mentioned, Miguel became pensive and quiet. "Well, Holy Spirit, what do you have in store for this young man and what is he hiding?"

"Well, lovely lady, I am praying for God's will about Ephesus, and I have a feeling that if Miguel gives us a ride north I know what we all should do from here. Lesia, you and your donkey can head for the Tyras River and young Ted can go with me since he needs to go back to his father and stepmother and let them know he is all right. What will happen is anyone's guess, but if God is in this, then we will have a great outcome."

Miguel and Ted

Miguel, fully recovered after a good night's sleep, finished the last of his sumptuous breakfast. "Breakfast was more than good. It was delicious and looking at beautiful woman was just an added pleasure. My dear lady, what will you be doing after I leave?" he commented to Lesia.

"Leave, sir, may I ask which way you are going?"

"After thinking about the purpose of my trip, I feel that if I'm up this far, I might as well check out the next island and even farther north if the weather holds," silently thinking about the blessing of the apron.

Lesia's heart jumped within her, and she gave the captain the best smile she had. "Kind Captain, I don't suppose you might consider taking a harmless woman on board who really needs to get to the Black Sea and up the Tyrus River, now would you?" she said, touching his hand.

"Well, why would you want to leave a lovely island like this?

What would your mother, Huldah, do without you?"

"No, no. I am not Huldah's daughter, just a traveler like you." Then she began to tell him about Mara Chin and Andrew and how she needed to try to find her mother and her siblings.

"Well, my lovely dove, you sure have had a time of it. You say that Andrew was a brother to Simon Peter. Did you know that he was in prison in Rome and caused a lot of commotion?

"I really don't know much about Peter except that Andrew loved him very much. They had lost their father and mother at a young age and were living with kinsmen. My life was the life of a slave, pushing back her hair and showing him the pierced earlobe."

"My chance at freedom came the night of the great fire. I was always busy helping my mistress Herodias with any of her demands at home or traveling back and forth from Jerusalem to Rome and other places. On that fateful day, we had just arrived in Rome, and once again, I was in high demand to help her get ready for Nero's grand party that night. We had arrived safely having a good voyage on a ship from Jaffa, but rushing to get to her villa, Herodias became like a mad woman. Back at the villa she kept trying to make herself the perfection of beauty, trying on one garment after another, throwing each cast-off garment at me, while at the same time, yelling at me that I would be whipped if she was late. Some of the bags were not even unpacked."

"After Herodias left, the fire began, so I ran for my life and found myself again onboard a ship that took me to Athens. In Athens, I met Bishop Ben, and well, kind Captain, I am boring you, but anyway, please, please, I feel you are my answer to prayer. The journey on your ship will save me days, even weeks, but I still have a little favor yet to ask?"

"Whatever it is, my lovely dove. If it will cause having you around for some more time, I shall be happy to say yes."

"Captain, I have a donkey! A donkey! Yes, a small animal, not a horse."

Miguel shrugged his shoulders, always a sucker for a beautiful woman. "It is the Spanish in me, a Spanish lover they call me! My dear, my ship does not carry animals, but if it is such a small donkey, what can I say but yes, but mind you, I will not take care of its shall we say needs," pulling her to himself to give her a big hug, but Lesia resisted.

"Oh, by the way sir, I don't know if you have ever been in love, but I was with Andrew, and every day he is still so precious to my heart," and at that a tear fell. Miguel was startled to see so great a love in evidence. The thought of these Christians again went through his mind, noticing the way they love.

Lesia took advantage of the moment as Bishop Ben entered the room. She blurted out, "Oh, Ben, you and Ted are going with me as far as Miletus where the captain will drop you off, right, sir?" A stunned captain's first thought was since when did he become a free ride, but on the other hand, he felt inside his heart that just maybe, mind you, Paul's God orchestrated the whole thing.

When Ted came in, Miguel's heart melted when Ted asked, "Do you have bulls and matadors in your country?"

"Why, yes, why do you ask?" Then the child began to tell him about his dream. Miguel grew quiet. He looked at the boy. "Son, why do you want to leave such fine parents with such great hearts?"

"Oh no, Captain, they are not my parents. I ran away from the farm because at the time I hated my stepmom, and my father always took her side. You see,

I love music, and they only were interested in work, work, work all day and all night."

"I see," contemplated Miguel, rubbing his chin and adjusting his chair. "Now let's see, what would you say to learning about work if you were to sail with me for one year? Mind you, it will be one full year, and you will find out what farm work and sea work are all about in this life. I was a lad like you when my uncle offered me the same choice. My family grew grapes and stomped them day and night. All day was not my choice," and on that note laughter broke forth from them both. "You will also get to see the beautiful city of Madrid with its beautiful women. At that, Bishop Ben began frantically clearing his throat quite loudly.

"Oh, could I, Huldah, Lesia, Uncle Ben, do this?" Ted pleaded.

The subject had been settled. Ted was to go back to Ephesus and talk to his family, a notable God-sky. Then Captain Miguel will be stopping on the way back to pick up Ted if and only if his parents agreed. Bishop Ben counseled, "Remember that you learned that to honor your parents is a promise for long life here on this earth. If God has a will for you, your parents also will know it and be sending you off with their blessings."

"So, Captain, we will be down at the ship after we pack and again say all our goodbyes." Shaking hands with Ben, Captain Miguel hugged Huldah and told Mara Chin he was a great chef.

Lesia sat stunned for a few minutes then it hit her. Father, and she ran into the kitchen to him. Saying goodbye is never easy even if it is for just a day, but Lesia knew that this was a journey maze starting up again. She had a little rest and a lot of loving from some great kids, but life continues to have challenges and changes, open doors, and closed windows. Her father tried to remind her of some events in her early life, but age and time had stolen a lot. Her necklace would at least be some identification, and now that they were all believers of God and His works, they knew that nothing is impossible with Him. "You find family, yes. Donkey help, yes, and Andrew's sandals comfort. You winner, no loser. No tears now, okie dokie. I happy first time. Love place and seeing you again. Love God's plans, yes, or else beautiful daughter, I long gone to ancestor's land."

Saying goodbye to the children was happy and sad. Alma Delores was excited that maybe Ted would be working on the Silver Eagle and would be her chaperon going back to Rome. Captain Miguel said he knew a friend, and he would not leave until Rita could follow up and find Paula and Anthony, especially Anthony, whose father works in the Senate. They were all satisfied with the outcome of the plan, a God-sky[10] working plan.

Miletus

Miguel was very glad that the docking at Miletus went smoothly, because of its shoreline.[11] Miguel acted as a tour guide for Lesia, both enjoying their sightseeing expedition of the small villages in the area. Her laughter was infectious, causing Miguel to ponder on Paul's words about settling down. Would he find someone like Lesia? A Christian? "Well, Paul, I am thinking."

Miguel helped with the donkey even getting it off the ship at Miletus and watching it do its comical turning around and around. Lesia also took the opportunity to witness to him. She told Miguel about Andrew talking to her about Jesus and how she would think, "Oh no, not me."

---

[10] when the handiwork of God knowing your plan, makes yours work out supernaturally

[11] research meander Miletus Meander: winding patter after the river https://www. bibleplaces.com/miletus/

"But there is something that draws on your heart strings. I know now that it was love for Andrew that was the most influential factor in the beginning. Then seeing his death, I was very angry at God, but seeing now how things are working out, I can see the bigger picture. Bishop Ben also influenced my thinking by talking to us about Paul's teachings regarding the mystery of God. It is just that: a mystery.

"I also began to recognize the miracle power on Andrew's sandals. It healed Paula's baby back in Athens, and when you go back, look at Alma Delores's face. Now as for the donkey, she found me, and her unusual actions have affected me, guiding me in certain directions to particular people, places, and things. I started calling these different happenings God-sky. When supernatural handiwork from God kisses my handiwork. Yes, you're smiling, but it's true. It's like you blink, and a God-supernatural event is there and has an influence over your life, giving you a miracle, then it is gone. The greatest miracle is that we have a chance to be God's child because of His great love—unfailing and unmerited.

"God provided this avenue back to Him by giving His most precious gift of love when He gave his only Son to die on that old rugged cross. I want to take this message back to my family and maybe continue doing what my love did: preach and witness about the Good News."

Miguel now was very quiet. Suddenly, he could not help himself. The last stronghold was abruptly broken by a soft voice coming from a gentle woman who witnessed that her beloved's death now drives her to a higher calling in her life. Rita had told him of the cruel treatment many Christians were experiencing. Now this too must be the high calling of God to make them willing to sacrifice themselves. Rita had also told him that she was thinking about being a believer. Miguel asked Lesia, "Was Paul the God-sky in my life? He preached the Good News to me so that I could make something worthy out of my life. I've been living by the physical flesh of wine, women, and song, but what will that give me in the end? Paul knew that he had a wild streak in himself and that it took an awful experience to knock him off his horse to wake him up. He asked me, 'Do you want God to knock you off your ship by sinking you and your crew?' That was a hateful statement from Paul, but now I hear it again through a woman's soft voice who loves forever." Come to me and believe in me and

I shall be your God was a message very strong on his soul and mind. Miguel took Lesia north as far as his ship and crew could manage in uncharted territory for them, but now he would go to Paul's apron and hug it to his bosom. He also realized that Samuel was a God-supernatural gift to him. He knew that he and his ship was blessed. The Silver Eagle flowed through smooth water created by the hand of God, and he recognized that a blessed future was in store for those who gave all their heart to the One who gave all His for them. "Rita, my dear, soon you shall be an honest woman," mused the newly enlightened Miguel.

Seeing the shoreline, Lesia was a little apprehensive and knew that here was where she would continue her journey, now with *her* being the focus of the ministry. As Miguel and Samuel managed to get that *little*-a hand higher than usual-donkey to shore, Miguel brings up to Lesia what she had told him about Ahava, just then Ahava does her antics making them both laugh.

Samuel was a sweetheart but soon began to show quietness, an unusual behavior for him, like his mind was somewhere else. He wouldn't answer when spoken to but kept looking around the area and out at the sea.

Lisa and Ahava watched now as the small boat pushed off, Samuel giving a mighty shove and Miguel adjusting the oar and pulling forcefully to overcome the incoming waves. As she continued to watch the progression of the boat, suddenly it appeared to have stopped in the water with both men enthusiastically talking to one another.

"I wonder what is going on?" she said aloud to Ahava. "Looks like they are just sitting there talking, but talking about what?"

"Captain?"

"Aye, man, what's up? You have been like a bull in a pen. Land life surely can't be the reason."

"Captain, can I say something?"

"Aye, man, but it better be important. I can feel the wind, and we need to be on board."

"Ye know that I have been grateful to you for paying me out of debtor's prison in Barcelona, the drinking and wenching and fighting. I have served you these long years now from youth into old age."

"Well, aye, go on."

Been sitting, looking around I'm homesick. Homesick! "Samuel, I knew a rat bit your leg, but now you sound like a beam hit your head hard. You stopped rowing to tell me you want to go home to Spain. Man, we are in the middle of the Aegean Sea. I am off course for the like of a damsel in distress, and now the crew is getting soft and still expects the same wages, and you are homesick. Do you think I can get us home in an hour?"

"No, ye see, look around ye Captain. I was born here in this area in a small village on the Black Sea. I ran away as a teen and ended up in Spain. Because I grew up in these parts, I knew where to go when ye ship was bound[12] to this area. I didn't know that ye knew the area, you dog! Ye never share this secret with me."

"The sweet lady also, her traveling alone. It isn't fair to her to let her set off in these parts by a hope in a donkey and a pair of sandals," stammered Samuel.

Captain looked around and then back to shore. Lesia and Ahava were still standing close together looking out at them. "Samuel, you're right. As badly as I hate to lose you right now, I sense in my heart that this was probably the reason you didn't die the night the rat chewed your leg." He put his hand into the side pocket on his tunic and pulled out a small coin purse. "Here, take this and help her as far as you can. Now tell me again just where is home."

"Ye can't see it from here, but there is a small village on the northern side of the Black Sea called Chersonesus. It's located at the southern end of the Crimean territory. I also have some relatives in Berea,

---

[12] Proceeding in a specific direction or to a specific place *outward bound—to leave the safety of port heading for the open ocean.

but they probably think I am dead. My brother Nicholas loved to drink and was a wild one."

"So, you had a brother and a family. Secrets, man."

"Bishop Ben is from the area, but I didn't recognize him, or he me. He could not recall anyone in Berea that had a name of Nicholas, but he did know about Paul. While at Miletus, I heard a rumor about someone called a one-eye preacher man no name though, had long ago preached there."

Miguel motioned for Samuel to row back to shore. When they arrived, Lesia hugged Miguel again and thanked him for Samuel. Once again, he took to the sea, but this time he rowed as one, while three stood on the shore and watched. Meanwhile Miguel was thinking of the way life had handled him for the past six months. Samuel would probably turn out to be related to the one-eyed preacher man. Wouldn't that beat all? From his meeting with Paul and Luke, he could hear them again saying, "Nothing is impossible with God."

Miguel pulled the last stroke and yelled to his crew, "Hoist me up. Pull in the boat and get ready to stand in order." He had to hasten now to pick up two kids. He was looking forward with enjoyment to teaching the boy the meaning of work on the open sea. Rome and Rita, then Barcelona. That was what his homesickness was about. As captain of the ship, he knew what he had to do. The crew recognized that vacation was over—spit and polish was at the wheel.

Black Sea

Samuel, Lesia, and Ahava started the walk with Samuel and Ahava taking the lead. Ahava began sensing right away that this man had a connection but was not quite sure if it was with Lesia or with the area. Samuel helped to make a fire that night, and with the blanket, he fixed a place for Lesia to get some rest. Ahava and Samuel also sat down close together by the fire. The stars illuminated the night sky and the weather was mild.

Ahhh, Samuel had almost forgotten the smell of land and her beauty with the wind blowing through the grass, giving the appearance of waves of water. He took his old, faithful, little knife and cut himself a piece of cheese. Huldah, he could have settled down with one like that and thought, *What a lucky man, Mara Chin, you old fox. I wonder what I will find when I get back home.*

He had finally met a reason for his life when he met Paul and Luke. Softly he began to converse with

Ahava, "Yes, Paul said all my sins—all my sins—are forgiven. He even stated that he was the chief sinner, killing women and children or throwing them into prison. Prison that was where Miguel found me. It was not the fortune I had so wanted out of life. Then there was the one woman I thought I could love, but instead, I abused her, so she had left me. Just my good fortune that she didn't die. Many others filled her place for a while, nothing lasting. Finally, I was thrown into prison, and while there, the captain came by inquiring about some extra rough men he wanted to hire, those who were unattached and had very strong backs. He told the guard that if some of these men wanted to work on the sea, he would pay the prison debt. I was one he asked about. Hearing the key unlock that gate was the beginning of my adventure with the captain. He paid my prison debt, and I was given the orders about no drinking on his time or my watch. What little change I did was for him, and I really owe him great thanks."

But then looking over at the sleeping woman, he wondered what she would find. Maybe it will just be like trying to find that mermaid that when young he always looked for—land people laugh.

He leaned back against Ahava, who grunted a little and soon the sound of sleep startled Ahava as her ears were sensitive. She lay in wonderment at the sound this human man makes.

When Samuel slid sideways, and his head fell on his jacket, Ahava slowly got up and headed toward the bushes where the angel was standing. Now Ahava had a new secret all her own. The early morning mist slowly arose from the seas, while the dew lingered yet on the grass. Soon the sun will raise high in the sky, giving warmth and beauty in a land unfamiliar to a woman who does not yet know her real biological family.

Yawing and stretching, Lesia remarked, "Well, I have had the comfort of a Roman's bed, and now the ground. Great going, Lesia, you have come up in the world," and on that thought she giggled.

Samuel hearing the giggle sat up and said, "Woman, what is so funny?"

"Oh, Samuel, I was just thinking. When my life was so comfortable, the grumbles kept coming out of my mouth. I guess people sometimes don't realize the difference between the times when they have it good and the times they have it rough."

"Ya, Miss, this ground is good compared to the filth of a prison floor, but I really miss the comfort of a loved one." On that he stood up and moved his aching legs to get the blood circulating. Age, getting older, where had his youth gone? He thought it would last forever then found out that life kicks a man right where he sits. What he doesn't know is that good was coming for him. His sister had never given up on him and has been looking for him every time she goes to the seashore.

Suddenly, they both realized Ahava was missing. Where was she? They called her name and turned to look if she had just strolled over to the clearing. Puzzled looks appeared on each face. They had to continue walking toward the Black Sea seashore to meet the fishermen coming in from the night runs to see if one might give them passage to his homeland. But what about Ahava? Samuel thought, "If Lesia wasn't looking, ye would be shot." Then Lesia broke that thought saying, "You know Samuel, Ahava has a strange way about her, a God-sky on her, so maybe she is involved in something right now. We will get started, and she will soon show up, trust me." Samuel grunted and thought, "First people, but now animals." However, he held his thoughts to himself. Then it hit him that while he attended to Ahava on the ship, he had stroked her ears and soon after his leg had stopped hurting. "Naw." He then shook that thought away quickly.

They began their journey to the Black Sea on a good, old worn path, where people from villages around had loaded their oxcarts or horses with goods to ship here and there for what they could receive in the way of wages: grain, wheat and corn, and vegetables from the fine soil, lovely grapes, good sheep with fine wool for spinning, fine cattle and horses. Little did they know what a surprise awaited them from both their pasts.

Samuel began to talk about his days spent with his brother walking the sandy shoreline. He grew up in the time of Rome's influence over all aspects of their lives: taxes, education, and life in general, which was both a blessing and a curse.

Samuel talked about the wolves, wild boar, beavers, and otters, which made Lesia a little more anxious about Ahava. He noted that the mixed trees made a lovely forest. His mother had told him about the different people coming from as far away as Egypt to settle in the Crimea area: the Aeolians, Durians, and Ionians. Also, moving into the area were Scythians and a group of nomads from north of the Black Sea, who were experts in horsemanship. We were glad for the diversity of people.

Samuel continued, "I wanted to see the world. Getting on that first ship was the beginning a big joy ride for me. I love the ocean and seeing the stars at night over the sea when the full moon would come out, and everything was harmonious with the captain and crew. However, life learned by experience can make you or break you. He expressed that having no education made him feel looked down upon when he saw anyone of the nobility and educated men of society. I was on the low rung of society. I wanted to own my own ship, but the grog and other things made me just one hand among many. He had witnessed births and deaths and different ways from different people.

"Everything changed for me when I learned from Paul about a new way of living. I learned that God loves me no matter what and that all my sins are forgiven; all I had to do was ask. I know inside my heart that compassion has entered." Looking at Lesia, he remarked, "It is important that I help you, as well as going back home with the Good News message."

I must find my brother, Nicholas, who also had a wanderlust spirit like me. Back years ago, Nicholas and I traveled together for a short time, we had quarrels, but this was the big one. I wanted to set out for myself. He choruses, "Young, Samuel was now going to see the world-to see the world; to make his fortune. The first job, ye find on any vessel sailing anywhere, anywhere, ye agreed to sign on. Stay here! ### ye listening! Stay here, no, ### big brother, ye are a rotten example-ye are the expert in loving and leaving and fighting. It is all that I can do to get along with ye."

Mug was right Lesia.

He shook for a minute remembering the whip being laid across his back, his young back which caused him to pause his speech for a moment, but he continued, now with old age and more wisdom, I am no longer full of anger toward Mug for trying to keep me close. I would hear news of him from time to time. Couldn't believe it, but Nicholas up and left his wife and kids as indentured slaves to Ernest, a tavern owner on the island Miletus.

On the sea, you learned how to throw a knife better than a bullet from a gun. In an evening drunken fracas, Nicholas had his nose smashed. From then on, he was called Mugface. He hated the name and fought everyone that remarked about it-until finally he accepted his looks."

Lesia couldn't understand the full impact of all the hurt and intensity of pain from what she was hearing about them but inside she heard their sorrow from their life, she could relate to some experience she had with old hateful. Love had been missing in Samuel, but finally finding the love of Jesus had melted the hard shell of a sailor into a sweet heart of a man.

They walked and talked and rested each day as they were waiting for Ahava to show up. But, no Ahava. At last, just as the sun was setting, and they came within sight of the beautiful Black Sea.

A small village appeared. Its houses were built of stone and wood with large hearth on the outer wall and blooming flowers in profusion. Smaller structures for animals were located farther down the worn paths. One stone house was bigger than the others and looked to Lesia like it was a main house for meetings or perhaps as Samuel suggested was probably used to hang the wares or skins for sale and probably held barrels for the salted fish. Samuel headed toward that building to inquire what or who was in with news about the area.

Samuel's thoughts lingered for a moment on his captain and the crew, and he wondered if Alma Delores would get to Rome and find her family. Little did he know that the crew was still in the Jesus mood, and with singing instead of cursing at the rising of sails, the journey was quite different. It was the best Christian ship afloat on the sea.

—∿—

Samuel entered the large, stone building. It was quaintly built with handmade wooden benches and tables and hanging skin booths. Lesia could smell the mixture of aromas, fruit to animals, and excused herself to step back outside. Samuel finally spotted the owner way in the back, arranging the potatoes along with some corn on homemade wooden flats. "Good evening, good man, how goes the day with ye?"

The man did not answer but just looked at Samuel with an inquisitive eye. "New here in these parts?"

"Yes," said Samuel, "but you see, I was born up north of the big sea and perhaps do not look like the young man that used to run these parts, but it seems like this building is also a new addition here. For right now, I need to get a ship or small barge to take the young lady and me home to Chersonesus." On mentioning that village name, the older man grinned and said, "Yes, welcome, and we do have a man who prides himself on doing good for others. We call him Preacher Man."

"Well, that will be fine with us," explaining his own religious renewal. "When shall Preacher Man arrive to this side of the shore?" "Oh, he is late right now, but if you just stick around, he will be here. You can trust him and his word. Yes, old Preacher Man has really made a lot of us believe that an evil one can change and become good. Now go over to my house and get Blandina to fix you and your daughter some tea."

Samuel smiled upon hearing Lesia called his daughter, a daughter he never stayed around long enough to claim, neither his women nor his offsprings. "May the God of heaven forgive and go forth to help the ones that were wounded and hurt by my selfness and stiff-necked heart," he prayed.

Meanwhile, Lesia wandered around looking and looking for a donkey that was now part of her life and who had apparently abandoned her and Samuel. She followed Samuel, who did not say anything but just walked toward another odd, round-shaped stone house. The paths were worn showing the connection between the two buildings. A smoke plume was rising through a stone like stack. After knocking using the big metal piece triangularly made, an elderly woman came, opening an odd-wooden door which was fixed to slide along the ditch dug earth that fastened around the bottom to secure the heavy size. *Clever*, Samuel thought. Then she recognized them as tired travelers, and with a grin and gesture of her hand, she welcomed them into her home, sliding the odd door closed. The smell of the fire was strong, yet the warmth was inviting, as well as the aroma of bacon being cooked along with a pot of vegetables.

On one of the homemade, small tables sat several black pottery jars of various sizes. Unusual they thought, yet they could not help admiring their beauty. Furs lay along the earthen floor, which gave another new experience for Lesia, compared to the Roman marble floors and round pillars. Taking a pot with hot water from the hearth, Blandina poured some into a large jar, stirred it, and then poured out good, strong tea into two small metal cups. Little conversation occurred to say the least as the dialect was different from Samuel's own town language, making it hard to understand. She made a gesture to pour another, but Samuel held up his hand and pointed toward the door. She acknowledged and slid open the odd door for them to go back outside.

Samuel remarked, "Things will be different as sure as we are standing here, Miss Lesia, for now we have witness these strange people from somewhere and their housing, have moved here." Lesia shook her head and just followed, still thinking how good the tea tasted and wondered how they came by it and if, maybe, there was some more in the other building.

Heading back to the large, stone building, Samuel spotted a big fishing vessel on shore. Amazing he recognized from the sails that the rigging was like the bigger vessels. This man knew his bigger ships.

He had just rigged the sails lower and used only two. Samuel stared at that new look and just shook his head wondering why he had not even thought of doing that to his small fishing boat years ago. Entering back inside the building, laughter was heard coming from the back. Then two men came forward as Samuel and Lesia were adjusting their eyes to the darkness of the room. Taller now and older, Mugface, still laughing and carrying a sack of potatoes, walked toward them. Then he froze and yelled, "Samuel, for the love of money and granny's nightgown, is that you, ye old buzzard and home wrecker. How, when?" He stood with an old, black patch over one eye.

Samuel, his senses beginning to return from the shock, thought, *How can this be? Am I dreaming? It can't be true. He was supposed to be dead. A shark somewhere, I heard.* His heart began to flutter faster so that they had to lay him down and let him get it together. His tears were too much for Mugface, and he too sat down and put his arms around Samuel. He joined in the wailing with tears and laughter. Lesia was crying, too, for she was wondering what it will be like when she sees her brother and sister for the first time, or maybe she would just be alone. She also knew that Andrew talked about how things were sometimes unexplained with Jesus, and miracles would take place. Now this family reunion she is watching. A reunion. Does this also mean God will reunite her because he also loves her?

Through his tears, Mugface muttered, "Ye old dog, wait until ye see the old homestead. Potamia never married as she took care of mother, and now we are living a short distance down the path. We have a small business here, bringing fish and other wares over to this side of the Black Sea. The bigger vessels come up the Aegean pathway, and so our larger wares including our cattle can be shipped for small earnings or used as barter.

"Let's go now," but Lesia interrupted Samuel.

"What about Ahava?" as she explained to Mugface about her donkey.

Samuel now coming to himself both mentally and physically said to Lesia, "We must leave. As you can see, this sea has a beach (sandy shoreline) around it, so the animal must fend for herself. Sorry little one, but if you believe that this donkey is a God-sky, then we must trust that belief. Like you said, it appeared out of nowhere. The fact of the matter did not go well with Lesia, but she knew to go hug Andrew's sandals and send up a prayer for herself and Ahava.

The three were soon sailing north along the shoreline toward another beautiful part of the Black

Sea and a village where the people and customs would unfamiliar to Lesia. The air was full of laughter as the two men renewed their friendship, reminiscing their childhood and thinking back to the time when they separated. Hugging each other several times on the journey, they were so glad that the God above gave them this wonderful opportunity to see each other again. Tears were mingled with silly reminders of how each had thought he was a gift to the world, especially to women. Lesia smiled as she heard that one.

Arriving to their destination, the men handled the boat, supplies, and fish they had caught like it was nothing at all. All were soon up at the house and wiping their feet. On side was a wash bucket supported by a giant size hook, with a dipper and fresh water. Each took a drink and poured some over dusty hands and rinsing off the grime of the journey. Samuel even wiped his face by pouring a dipper full of water over it. Laughing as they open the door, they gave a yell like they did in their childhood. Potamia came hurrying to the entrance room and seeing them began wiping her eyes. Now there were three going on and on and on. Lesia wondered if she would experience some of this joy exhibited by the reuniting of brothers when she finally found her siblings. Samuel's experience had made her realize that someone bigger is taking care of mankind. God does look down through the sky and watches the earth he created.

Finally, everyone took notice of Lesia and began hellos and introductions. After explaining how and where she would sleep, all three asked her lots of questions. Time slipped into evening with everyone sitting down to supper of fish, rice, and fresh fruit with wine and juice to drink. Soon the weary travelers lay down to rest for the night, sleep coming easily.

Morning brought a few chickens running through the house, which startled Lesia, and she began to wonder if she had made the right choice to travel to this unknown and uncharted territory. She then wondered what Old Hateful would have done with chickens having free range in the palace, which made her laugh thinking back to the reaction displayed to just an old ship's cat.

She finally caught sight of the fur ball that had been sleeping just across the floor. What! She froze, but the animal just stretched and darted away toward the front of the house.

The house was built with Roman-style influence of huge stone-work with odd pillars and the look of several chambers ahead of time and rich and poor looking to Lesia. The stones mud pillars doing the decorative strength separation along with adding privacy, and sturdiness, for the tall wood and high beams crossing from stone pillars to pillar. It had a hearth in the kitchen area that could hold several black pots at one time. The table was rustic but had a weaving cloth long enough to cover it plus hang over at the ends. A small container of Turkish coffee[13] set on the end of the table.

These strange items and ideas were introduced to his wife and Potamia. He had learned of them when on the island from a Captain whose ship came from Joppa, carrying a traveler from the famous Trade Route[14] called the Silk Road. Mugface bought gifts[15] and spent hours gleaning ideas for the home place.

After his salvation experience, Mugface went back to Miletus to pick up his family and return to his birthplace at Chersonesus. He and his wife came here to be near his sister. He was sorry that he was too late to kiss and tell his mother about his meeting John Mark and to show her the scribbles of the Word from St. Peter himself. His other gift was to show her his healed eye.

Mugface wished he could see John Mark just one more time. He would thank him again for the day he

---

[13]   **coffee came from Ethiopia, Yemen

[14]   *it is a cultural bridge between Asia and Europe.

[15]   ***I Kings Chapter 10, (Queen of Sheba) who brought spices and gold and precious stones to Solomon.

came aboard the old merchant ship. Since that time, He and his family have been so happy. He had built a good trading building and established a successful business. Now that his family was together again, he had a great big dream, his children will help him succeed in business, marry, and provide him with grandkids. The dream goes on and on.

Potamia set a couple more plates at breakfast as Mugface and Callidora (gift of beauty) and children were coming over. They were excited to see Samuel and Samuel gave Calla a hug well beyond deserving for forgiving a hot-headed brother but taking him back. He shook his head at all the children and looked with love at a new Mugface.

Everyone now especially the children turned their interest to the tall, beautiful woman from Rome. Nicholas II, Alexis, Lauren, Caity, and Eunice all were so warm and friendly that Lesia thought this could be a family for me, especially for right now.

Nicholas II was the oldest and quietest, and Lesia wondered if he should have Andrew's sandals. She kept this thought hidden for now, waiting for revelation in due time. But in the meantime, her thoughts lingered on Ahava. The donkey was extremely missed since she was part of Lesia's life now as well as part of the puzzle that was still not connected.

Lesia leaving right away was put to a vote, the answer—a great big no. For now, they wanted to hear about her life and her adventures along with Samuel's. The *no vote* inside made her have a moment thinking *I'm still a slave.* Later she realizes they had her best interest at heart.

Rome was a nice rest and Alma Delores was also an excited young believer. She was with Paula LaRosa and fell in love with that baby boy. They were still looking for her brother and mother, but everyone was hopeful of finding them.

Rita soon was packing, and Ted helped carry her belonging to the captain's quarters. A simple marriage ceremony occurred on board ship. Miguel pronounced, "My dear, with Paul's apron tied around your hands, this is a forever." Ted provided a lovely, sweet tune, and Miguel realized the boy's gift. Miguel's aunt was a music lover and gifted also. Now he must let Ted become one of Spain's best musicians and with his gifted aunt, he did not have to hire any teachers.

Planning the next step for Lesia's travel, time began to pass by quickly.

Mugface told of his experiences with John Mark, who was instrumental in his salvation and his healing while on a voyage from Rome where John Mark played a tough sailor. He also had Peter's Jewish cap.

Lesia realized that she too had known John Mark, the young man she had met in Jerusalem along with his wonderful mother. Everyone had begun to recognize that Mugface's experience had far-reaching implications, greater than what they could see in their little group. They continually asked God's blessing on their extended family as they daily knelt on skin rugs on the earthen floor to praise the One who loved them.

Mugface and Callidora had already started a small home group with the few people that were open to coming, and when they heard the stories, they spread the word so that the group had now grown to about twenty. The kappa, Peter's cap, was a great story for a laugh; however, when Mugface removed his black patch to show his healed eye, well, what can be said? The reality is far more than words can tell.

The day arrived when Mugface was to set sail for the Sarmatia area (modern Ukraine) and toward another unmapped journey for Lesia. After assembling a package of supplies and food, Mugface and his older son Nicholas II both said they would be going with her and would stay one day to find out which way would be best to start her journey. They wished that Lesia's donkey was there to help her. It would be one way to ease her journey by carrying her possessions and allowing her to ride part way.

Mugface considered bartering with one of the residents for a good *old* horse, so Potamia gave Lesia some older pants of Nicholas, which she could put on under her skirt to make riding Grey a little more comfortable. She had learned about this technique from a nomadic group up north that herded horses.

The sun was out, and the warmth felt good to the face and on the arms. The boat ride over to village on the mouth of the Southern Bug (Hypanis). Mugface went over the story that Lesia gave him from Mara Chin. He recognized that this would be like looking for a minnow in an ocean. Yes, God will have to send a miracle to this young lady. He thought that the Mara Chin family could have come through Kamians'ke village, which would be near the Borysthenes River and on that he had a hunch he had it right. They could have come down to Tyras (Odessa) and kept going south and that way brought them north of Greece. She could retrace their steps by going east toward the Olibia, which is at the mouth of the Hypanis River. Yet she knew that her necklace was pure gold and was maybe the work of a group called Scythians. Still puzzled, he kept his thoughts to himself and prayed a sincere, long prayer under his breath.

Ahava

The angel had sent Ahava on a mission, and now she was heading for the little villages near the Borysthenes and Olibia located at the mouth of the River Hypanis.

A trapper had found her, or shall we say Ahava found him because he would be Lesia's guide, getting her to where she should be. The angel would appear then disappear at various times on her journey; however, now she had not seen Him for some time and was wondering where the exact connection to her mission for Lesia will be as a lot depends on what Lesia is doing herself.

The next morning Ahava followed the angel and found herself at the mouth of Hypanis River (Olbia), taking in the sights and sounds of all the small groups bartering and traveling.

Ahava's ears picked up the noise coming from the wharves and fishing vessels. The children and wives of the fishermen were on the sandy shore line greeting the arriving fishermen who had gone out to catch a haul for their livelihood. Ahava looked at each woman. No Lesia, and then she heard Lesia's laughter as she jumped into the water along the edge or rather slipped and got her feet and skirt wet. Nicholas jumped out of the boat thinking Lesia was going to go in the water headfirst, and he didn't even know if she could swim. Now with two wet travelers and a hot day, Lesia thought, *Okie dokie. Right, Father?* The sun would do its job drying us out.

Lesia didn't see Ahava clopping along slowly toward this extraordinary scene. Ahava thought, "Just leave Lesia alone for a short time, and she gets into trouble. Now look at those rough ones with her, and where is Samuel?"

"Come, Old Grey, I am the one to get you ashore. Easy, girl, now up on the bank," said Samuel. Samuel from a distance spied Ahava and was beside himself. He rubs his scar on his leg.

Mugface then saw the donkey and let out a yell that startled the nearby fishermen as they looked up to see what was going on. Lesia eyed him. "What in the world is wrong with you, Mugface?"

"God did it," he yelled. "God did it."

Then Lesia started running toward Ahava. "Oh, my loved one, were you ever missed. Yes, God did it," she said, hugging the neck of Ahava and stroking her hand over Ahava's back. She noticed then that Ahava's belly was somewhat swollen. "What? Mugface, what do you think?"

"Don't know, milady, not quite an expert on animals, but didn't you say a little donkey? Don't think so." Then the people saw the crazy yeller now laughing. Yes, all were laughing. Some just shook their head. Strangers, so they just ignored them.

Lesia thanked Mugface and Nicholas and Samuel and waved to them as they reset to sail toward home.

Ahava, with her back loaded and Lesia trying to settle herself on the comfortable Old Grey, gently as a kitten, slowly started the final journey toward the farm known only for now by Ahava.

Ahava listened, and yes, she could hear the trapper that she had met earlier in her personal mission, bargaining at a table full of wares. She wondered if he was concerned when she was gone the next morning. He was very intent in what he was now doing. Talking to another man in skins, something about his first pet.

Great, she thought with her memory of that black wolf attack.

That was enough for me in this wilderness.

The night had been cool, and as the trapper, Asher, and Ahava were bedding down by the fire. Trapper's pet she-wolf began to growl, the hair standing up on her back. The trapper pulled out an arrow and sat very quietly when out of nowhere a big black he-wolf sprang for his she-wolf. The trapper jumped up and let the arrow fly, but it pierced both animals. The penetrating silence was dreadful as he cradled his pet; then with a roar, he began beating his chest in a ritual of mourning. Trapper then kicked up the fire and started several more, placing himself and Ahava in the middle for safety. Then the angel appeared, and Ahava knew that the scare was over. Then left him.

Ahava headed more toward a path which was to leave where they were now and begin heading for home. When she came in sight of the trapper, she brayed. He turned around and grinned. "Well, I see you have found another lost traveler, and it looks like she doesn't know much about riding a horse. Let me introduce myself, lovely lady." Lesia was attempting to adjust herself on the saddle got off and was going to remount the horse. "May I show you which side to mount your horse, while looking again, at the familiar donkey."

The saddle was old and a larger size made for an old work horse. Smiling, he thought this is going to be some journey, slow. Lesia looked at him with distrust. The men in her life at least showed arms and legs, remembering the Roman soldiers, but this one had a skin coat and dirty shirt, and an animal hanging from his head. If she could have run, she would have, but run where? "Oh Andrew, Andrew, what is going to happen to me? Please my darling, love, look from heaven and send me help." She looked at the arrows on his back and the two knives on each side of a cloth belt. "I know he is a man, but is he trustworthy?"

The new pet hidden in his backpack then let out a whimper. He had bartered for a puppy! "Here, my lady, let's have this little one ride behind you as there is plenty of room in this saddle."

"Hmm… I think he smells and is making a pass at me," and suddenly she felt like letting her foot slip a little, kicking trapper almost right in the face. How wrong about him she will soon discover.

Ahava, noticing the touché action, decided it was time to get this journey on the move, so she began to head toward the old trail that would lead up along the big river in a northerly direction. "My lady, I am also heading north," the trapper advised. Wondering how the spooky donkey and the horse and a beautiful woman connected. Ahava brayed like, "Well, so are we." Somewhere along the way, the trapper will take another route, but for now he is part of this triad.

Ahava

Ahava knew that Lesia's brother Bohdan had married Nadia and moved to the outskirts of Zhytomyr, and this is where he was to bring Lesia to be back home, then mission one would be complete.

Mission two, well that was yet to come. Would it be more with the trapper? The angel had her with this young man and again he is in the triad. So far, with him he is a lover of wolves.

Hidden Identity

Jordan Cohen son of Catherine and Giorgos Cohen, Jordan means *farming man* changed his name to Tanner—tanner of animal skins others just referred to him as trapper his life kept close to his vest since he lost his pet and the woman he loved. The trapper and Lesia were getting along better as she realized that all her learning did not include building fires in the woods, finding fresh water, or fishing in the river. The fish he cooked was delicious. Realization and now respect came quickly having this fur-looking young man along on this journey turned <u>out to be a</u>

<u>great blessing</u>! She was a bit surprised at this side of her personality, quite opposite of the delicate lady dressed up in a Roman toga, hardly ever getting her feet dirty much less her entire being. She found that with her skirt gone; she had gained more freedom for riding in the big, old saddle.

The puppy was growing and was as cute as could be for a wolf cub. She never really had the time for animals before though she loved kittens. She began to listen to when it whimpered and stopped to let it down on the grass, laughing as it sniffed everything, enjoying its antics, and crying out when its tail almost got the foot of Old Grey on it. "You better get back up, little one. You are a very curious one for a pet. Trapper, are you really sure this is the kind of pet for you?" She did not know that his lack of response was not rudeness but sadness as he thought of how his one careless moment cost the life of a loving, faithful one.

Her back after so many days on Old Grey began throbbing. After supper, she said, "Tomorrow I will be walking, kind trapper. My backside is turning into leather."

He laughed and then stated, "With that, we better rearrange some things. We can take some things off Ahava and put it on Old Grey, giving Ahava a break from being the only pack donkey."

She laughed and began to pet the pup. "And may I also remind you that the animal will be going with me when we part." *What a meany*, thought Lesia, but he is right. She was getting involved, and it would really be rough to see it go. She felt at times she was a slave again, but knew that out in this new wilderness each had to pull his weight.

Ahava rolled in the grass and brayed her bray for *silence* had been too long and needed to be gone.

The trapper had with good archery several ducks out of the sky and was now preparing them on a makeshift pit with an unusual odd pan he placed across the flames. Interesting, she had never eaten outside so much nor had she eaten animals killed and cooked on the spot.

Life certainly had turned out differently than what Lesia imagined it would be. She sighed and wondered, noticing her hands, what it would have been like if she had stayed with Mara Chin and the children. Then she began to prepare the area where they would sleep that night. As she began to clear stones and sticks and even pulled on some weeds, again looking at her hands, and then her shoes, she was glad that Samuel had given her a pair of Mugface's daughter's shoes. They were thicker than the open-toed sandals of Rome, made of cowhide and the covered the whole foot; however, they were not as flexible as her sandals. She tried pushing and kicking some of the rocks out of her way, but noted that the shoes didn't stop the pressure upon her toes when she slammed her foot into a large rock. "Ouch, I felt that all the way to my brain."

Looking around, Lesia thought that she had done a very good job even if she had to say so herself, and just in time as trapper was returning with a sack of fresh berries. Thinking to herself, "Gosh, what does this man not know? Yes, Andrew, I can see you eating this way as you traveled." And on that note, she pretended that he was beside her and was enjoying her taking pleasure in this new adventure. She was once again focused on what her main purpose was, and if chance had not intervened in her early life, this would be where she would have learned and lived and possibly have been a married woman with children.

Lesia was startled when the trapper opened and began to converse with her. "Lesia, I am a trapper, and I have traversed this wild, unsettled territory for weeks on end, hunting the wild and untamed animals for their pelts, plus I also tan hides, so people started calling me Tanner. That is what I answer to now. I live with my mother, but my father passed away many years ago. My father was skilled in wood working, but somehow traveling the wilds excited me more. Aloneness has caused me to be somewhat of a loner, you might say. Sorry if I come across with impatience, but you are unskilled, my lady, and I am very surprised that you have ventured out into the unknown with just a donkey and a pair of sandals that you seem to rely on. I am very puzzled."

Tanner then began to question her about the sandals. On that one, Lesia hesitated. She knew that he must be aware they were men's sandals. How would she begin to tell him about a love that was at this moment refreshed just minutes ago in her thoughts? She finally began with the story of living in Jerusalem: the people, the area, Mara Chin, and her Mistress Queen Hateful, which she didn't say out loud, but called her Herodias, the wife of King Herod. Tanner restoked the fire and let her continue on and on.

Lesia cried and laughed, and Tanner realized the sheltered life she led and was a little bit sorry for coming at her so hard when she grumbled. He realized she was a real tenderfoot. He held up his hand, showing that it was time for sleep, but really, he just could not bear anymore of her story or her emotions. He also lost one that he had loved, and as of now had not found another woman to replace her. Replacing a loved one was not as easy as replacing his old she-wolf Asher (meaning happiness).

He also wondered about this Jesus she talked about, the one that Andrew had left to serve. His religious knowledge came from his great-great-grandfather, who told him that the angel Michael was their protector as he was in an old story about a man whose name was Daniel. They had left their homeland to explore more religious freedom to get away from people who sacrificed their children on a fire to a worthless, lifeless statue. Sleep finally came and soon Ahava's unexpected mission would begin about two hours into their next day's journey.

Tanner awaking first as always, and after a short trip away from the camp he came back and began loading up the animals, then remembered that Ahava was to be free today of any burden on her back. Old Grey seemed happy enough with her load, and the pup on top shifting back and forth was a funny picture. They ate some hard, dry meat as Tanner checked all his knives. He then took the arrow bag and placed it on Old Grey.

Ahava started out in step with them and then would spot a nice bit of grass farther ahead or to the side and with the freedom to go she would head for it and then cantor back to walk again beside Lesia.

Then suddenly she stopped. Picking up a groaning or a cry of some sort, she looked around and then held up her head with her ears pointed as best as they could get. She then listened and listened. Braying forth a curdling bray, which startled Tanner. She took off toward an obscure path. Tanner yelled, "Hey," and then he let out a whistle that startled Lesia. "What in blazes is that crazy animal doing that she headed east toward that village? We are still going north."

Then Lesia told him that Ahava's change in behavior and her actions means something. Ahava suddenly did not come back but stopped for a moment, and she brayed again before she headed toward the village. "We've got to follow her. Tanner, it is a gut feeling."

The sounds increased, so Ahava knew that it was the right direction. She looked back to check if Lesia and Tanner were following, and yes, they were. At that moment, the angel appeared briefly and then was gone. Soon she arrived at the village where she found several small and large homes, some wooden and some stone, arranged in an orderly fashion.

Ahava passed several and headed toward a smaller cottage with smoke coming out of the chimney. She now knew it was a woman or child that was in some sort of pain. Tanner ahead of Lesia was about to hand slap a rope around Ahava's neck when he heard the scream of a woman. He dropped the rope and knocked on the door.

"Hello, are you okay," he yelled. Then when he heard the scream again. He just opened the door, which to his surprise was unlocked.[16] There in the back corner was a woman giving birth. She acknowledged Tanner by the wave of her hand and with heavy breathing said her husband had left to go get the neighbor girl, Phoebe. Then she fell back onto the straw mattress. Tanner was gifted in these things being instructed by his mother, who took him with her when the village women gave birth. He quickly went to the hearth and put his knives into a pot of water to cleanse them. Lesia slowly walked into the cottage. Never having seen childbirth, the sight was almost a horror picture of a raging woman. *Young*, she thought. What's wrong?" she asked Tanner. Tanner again realized how uneducated Lesia was about many practical matters.

"A baby, woman, a baby. Now get over to that small piece of cloth and begin to tear me some small strips. What? Yes, small little strips," and then he grabbed the cloth and showed her how to tear the first strip. Her hands were trembling as she began to do this, while the woman's groaning caused her to flinch. Tanner knew that the youth of the woman was going

---

[16] Latch lifters bolted door from the inside, this one was off.

against her, and the baby was breach. Lesia picked up the worried looked on Tanner's face. He now was stepping away to wipe the sweat from his forehead. "Mother, how I wish you were here."

He went and mixed water with a little powder he always carried in his bag and had the woman drink some to ease the pain. Tanner withheld information about the baby being breach since this seemed to be the young woman's first birthing experience. Ahava heard again the moans, so she brayed loudly. Lesia went out to see what Ahava was braying about and why she was acting so differently now. She found Ahava holding Andrew's sandal in her mouth. "What? Oh, yes, Ahava," remembering Paula's baby boy. She grabbed the sandal and quickly returned into the cottage and headed back to the bed. Tanner seeing the sandal wondered what this woman was doing now. He thought one woman out of her mind was enough. Lesia placed the sandal on the woman's stomach. The woman was ready to knock it off when a sudden movement inside her caused her to become quiet. Tanner then checked her again. The birth canal showed the crowning head. "May the God of Andrew be blessed, and thank you Michael who was his mother's belief, be blessed, Ahava be blessed. Lesia be blessed, and please steady my hands," he said to himself.

Just then in walked Christine's husband, John, and Phoebe just in time to see a big, beautiful, baby boy come into the world. He then helped Tanner cut the cord, all the while smiling from ear to ear. He then said to Tanner, "You must be like a doctor, but why the sandal?"

Tanner just laughed and said, "You will have to ask Lesia, but for now, we must move Mama and get rid of the old straw bed and put in another. So now, man, show us where to take this." Tanner then noticed Phoebe, who was pretty and about his age. She began the process of cleaning and swaddling the baby and getting him ready for his first dinner. Tanner could not for some reason keep himself from looking at Phoebe. He had not been attracted to a woman for years since losing Junia. What he did not know was that the blessing of the sandal was also at work in two people's hearts.

Tanner now believed the stories that Lesia had shared at the campfire, and he also wondered about his own heart if he wanted to serve this new God that she called Jesus. The journey was now delayed as Phoebe and Lesia began to fix a good supper. The sound of frying chicken could be heard and the aroma of fresh fruit for a salad filled the small cottage. However, as Tanner observed, Lesia taking the outer layers off quite nicely on those potatoes.

—m—

Lesia later hugged Ahava and confirmed by whispering into her ear that now she was so glad she was different and then thought of Andrew's sandals. "You are a part of helping me, and though I don't completely understand all of this just now, you and the sandals have a connection, but some mysteries like God-sky belong only to God himself."

Tanner suggested that he accompany Phoebe home because he wanted to meet her father. They were stepping outside when Phoebe's father came into the yard. "I thought, daughter, that you would need someone to escort you home." She smiled and hugged him. She then introduced him to everyone and began explaining what had just happened and that she stayed longer to help prepare a meal. "You are your mother's daughter child. But did you say something about a sandal that was worn by Andrew?"

"Yes, Father. Lesia and Tanner were coming home with me so that they could tell you all about it."

"Well, let us go then." He then asked Lesia why she had Andrew's sandals. If she had known she would have delayed the answer, for as soon as she said she witnessed Andrew's death and the elderly couple gave her the pair to give later to a worthy man, Ezar Rubin cried out, beat against his chest and tore his shirt, while falling to the ground. She and Tanner were caught off guard and were afraid at first that Phoebe's father was having a seizure. Phoebe waved her hand indicating that they wait a minute then she too went down on her knees beside the sobbing priest and joined him in Jewish custom of deep sorrow.

Tanner went to comfort Phoebe, and Lesia joined them when she realized they were weeping and mourning Andrew. "Oh my, they have met him and have loved him," and with that she let her tears flow. She mourned for him herself, a final mourning that had gotten shoved deep inside as she had moved on with her own problems.

Ahava could even hear the low sobs and moved away toward Old Grey that was beginning to act agitated with her load and the pup playing around her legs. Ahava took her reins into her mouth and headed down the road for she knew that they were going to be here for a few days. It would take that long to explain the miraculous story. So, she thought that she and Old Grey might as well go and get settled down, and hopefully, someone would soon be there to unload the horse.

Arriving at the larger wood and stone cottage, Ahava let out a good hello bray. Phoebe's brother came out to check upon the ruckus. *Young man*, Ahava thought, *please unload Old Grey. She is about to roll, and the supplies, which are not much, will be rolled in the grass.* Jacob looked and began to unload the old horse, knowing that animals are also supposed to enjoy the Sabbath, as well. As he stroked the old horse, he began to talk to her, "You are a little sweaty, old girl, so you have earned yourself a rest time." He then proceeded to walk them back to a small stable area. *Ahh, water to drink and hay. Thank you, thank you,* thought Ahava. No one had to coax either animal to get right to work filling their hungry bellies.

Jacob studied both for a moment then he stroked Ahava, remarking, "Young lady, you sure have reminded me of another donkey who had a similar coloring as you." He would later learn that there was more to that idea that he could ever imagine. Rabbi Ezar silently stood then started for home with the rest following. Little did he know that a young father and mother were watching the whole affair, wondering if it had to do with the preacher man that had even visited them. John hugged Christine and said, "what would you think if we call our baby boy Andrew?" They turned to go directly to the child and with great joy lifted baby Andrew and blessed God, the God that they had rejected years ago when Andrew preached the Good News. Right at this moment, they believed and promised their child that they would be the Christian parents that Andrew talked about, those who loved with all their hearts and with all their souls. Andrew had talked about salvation as a gift. It took a baby as a sky gift that made them surrender their souls to Yeshua. Christine wondered what would have happened without their miracle, Andrew's sandal and on that note the couple just hugged each other and their child as tears of gladness rolled down both faces.

Meanwhile, Jacob met his father, sister, and two strangers as he came around the corner of the cottage. "I put a horse and a donkey in the stable around back," he announced. "Are they yours?" Lesia and Tanner just shook their heads when they realized how they both had forgotten about the animals, and even the she pup was left on her own. Now though, they were waiting with excitement to hear how and when Ezar had met Andrew.

Phoebe quickly excused herself and went to her mother, explaining briefly why she had not been back for Sabbath. Lesia and Tanner soon realized that they too had entered the quiet and rest time, so they had no choice than to relax and meditate within their own souls. Soon, however, Tanner was snoring, and Phoebe had to giggle softly as she took Lesia to her own room. "Father will talk to us in the morning. He was very much moved. You see, Andrew was like an older son and Father loved him in that way. Andrew knew he was welcome here whenever he would return from taking the Good News message to other places. He knew that rest and food was his for the asking." Soon she blew out the candle and left Lesia to her own thoughts.

"Andrew, oh, Andrew, the sandal. It helped bring a miracle for that young couple, and Andrew, it was a sweet baby boy." With that she placed the sandal behind her pillow and would hear for the first time music of many countries floating through space and time.

Ezar and Dell Rubin were smiling as sunshine was again crossing the east windows, and it was going to be another beautiful day in their lovely home. Jacob, their wonderful son, had already gotten up and gone to see to the sheep, chickens, and of course, the two or shall we shall three new visitors. She pup chewed at his leggings, and finally Jacob picked her up and put her high in the nest of one of the chickens. She looked out and with a whimper wanted down, but Jacob would not comply until the straw was replaced and water was put into each water trough. Finally, he put she pup down, who then followed him back to the house.

You are a very playful animal, he thought, but wondered what his older sister Phoebe and her cat would think.

Tanner was coming down the path and asked what he could do, but Jacob told him that all the morning work was finished. He did wonder, however, what to do with Mischief here. Tanner laughed. "Well, son, she was to be left to grow somewhat wild, but Lady Lesia started right away domesticating her with ear scratching and holding. There's no time like now to introduce a small change of lifestyle. She could be introduced to a soft leather lease," and on that he removed his waistband and gently put it around the pup's neck, and then the pup was placed beside a small bush with water and a nice leg bone to chew on.

"*Boruch ato elohoynu melech ha-olom ha'motzeh lechem men ha'aretz* (Blessed are you O Lord, Our God, King of the Universe, who brings forth bread from the earth)." Tanner, Jacob, and Rabbi Ezar retired toward the middle room furnished with specially made old chairs, covered with embroidered cloths made with a horizontal needle woven design. The women began to clean up the kitchen and soon joined the men.

Who will go first? thought Lesia, but since she already knew her story, she was anxious to hear Rabbi Ezar. When he smiled, warmth flowed out from this man.

"My children, it is a long story of how we ended up here, and while here, we have very carefully kept our faith secret. One day it was raining and coming down by the bucketful. To my old eyes what did I see as I was running toward the house but a donkey braying at me? Afraid of the animal, I was just about ready to hurl a stone at it when I hear, 'Don't please.' The donkey was faster than I since she bolted at the crack of the thunder, and I found myself on the ground. "'Kind sir, may we find some shelter in your barn, and as soon as we can we shall move on.'

"Both were soaked so I asked, 'Did you not seek shelter along the way man?'

"He replied, 'I wanted to, but Malka would not see to it.' I was puzzled by that answer. Since when should a donkey boss its owner? "Well, by now my clothes were soaked. We hurried to the door of the house but were greeted with, 'Stop, you two. Drip right where you are! Jacob, get some rags from the closet and bring a robe for your father. You, stranger, will have to disrobe, and Jacob will bring you a blanket.' My wife shook her head noting that a drowned rat could not have looked worse. She remarked, 'This young man needs some meals in his stomach.'"

Andrew stammered while warmth met chill, and his goose bumps ceased soon after he was wrapped in a lovely blanket. He and Rabbi were warming themselves by the big kiln inside with a good, hot fire going and a strong, hot cup of tea. A pair of Jacobs's pants was found for Andrew, but the shortness caused his ankles to look very lonely with his size feet.

Dell had taken all the clothes to a tub out back that Phoebe had filled with good, hot water, plopping Andrews's clothing in to be cleaned and rinsed. A rainbow briefly appeared then soon the storm was over. Good, old sunshine and wind quickly dried his clothing, while after finishing a full meal, he found himself asleep on Jacob's bed. He slept through until evening, and Ezar extended his hospitality for he noted that Andrew had a drive or mission. Jacob remarked that the donkey had helped herself down at the barn, and Old Goat even was getting along with her, which was refreshing since Old Goat hated any animal that wanted to share his oats.

"Well, one day went into two and then into weeks. Andrew became like a member of the family. He told us of his call to spread the Good News of Jesus. He had been to many places, preaching to many groups of people. Some understood the message but others he ministered to by drawing pictures.

"His faithful donkey had a God-given purpose, and he told us many stories about how she would take the lead to find a person or a group of people needing help, and some of those he met needed healing or a great miracle. Andrew then started to tell of his childhood, and his brother Simon. He also spoke of John the Baptist, then Salome, James, John, and the Sea of Galilee, his beloved sea and its people. He mentioned that Jesus, a Jewish rabbi, chose twelve apostles, but one of the twelve betrayed Him, so Jesus was killed on a Roman cross.

"He talked about one he found whom he loved, but the call to preach and the love he had for Jesus caused him to choose to become a eunuch and follow the Calling wherever it took him." He stopped to look at Lesia, and she knew that it was now time to add her story. "Yes, he sold fish in Jerusalem and brought some for my father Mara Chin." She then went into the fish story, causing everyone to laugh and then said that was when love was born. "Andrew talked and talked about his group and this Jesus that it was plain that he really believed this new teaching. It was then that

I explained about the slave-ring in my ear, and told Andrew that he wore an invisible Jesus ring in his ear."

Lesia recounted the story of Herodias causing the head of John the Baptist to be brought to her on a plate, but that later when the uprising began and she felt danger Herodias hurriedly went to Rome, taking me with her. She explained that they lived in Rome many years, and then visited Jerusalem once again. But as Herodias was in the habit of habitual action, she decided once again to return to Rome.

"The six-day fire in Rome set me free, so I left Rome and eventually arrived in Athens. There I met Bishop Ben, who told me that he had heard that Andrew was in Patras, so we both walked there; then he departed to go find some new converts in the area for some wanted to learn about baptism. While I was working one morning, some sailors came into the tavern, and I was direct in asking them if they had heard or seen a preacher man. I was told that Andrew was seen three days ago in a village north toward the sea. A gut feeling caused me to leave the tavern.

"I headed for the small village, and was met by people rushing up the path, so I followed them and found a crowd that were watching a man hanging on an X-shaped cross. I asked who it was and what was going on.

"One of the watchers said, 'Oh, my soul, they are killing the preacher man.'

"At that Ezar saw and felt the horror of the scene, so he said, 'Child, let's finish this later. Right now, we will finish the chores and then eat supper. You help Phoebe with supper, while us men will do the chores.'" Leaving the room, Lesia found herself in Phoebe's arms expressing loss again, time seeming to stop.

Tea and the lighted candles were so comforting, and Lesia was enjoying the Shema, recited every day at 8:00 a.m. and 8:00 p.m. "*Sh'ma Yisrael Adonai Eloheinu Adonai Ehad* (Hear o Israel the Lord is our God, the Lord is One)."

Lesia now understood how Andrew could relate to this family. They had Jewish roots and were kind, loving, and very giving to him. His Jesus was Jewish and was so kind, he gave his life for all sinners. "Oh, Andrew, God bless you, my love," and she again touched her ear and remembered the kiss so sweetly given to her so many years ago.

"*Boruch ato Adonoy, Elohaynu melech ho-olom, boray p'ri hagofen* (Blessed are you, O Lord, our God, King of the universe, who creates the fruit of the vine)." The wine was good and Tanner now knowing that Phoebe was Jewish had to do some rethinking about her. Yes, yes, his background was close, but he and his mother were not keeping the full Torah since his father died, yet he had enough teaching that a man who does good will be blessed back with good. Normally, the full story about a Jewish man dying on a cross would have been rejected, but how could he deny the miracle with the sandal and the man who wore it. Lesia had told him that by faith we believe and that salvation is a gift.

He looked around the room then went out back to talk to Jacob. "Jacob, what would you say if I spoke to your father for your sister's hand?"

"What, that would be great. I admired how you handled the emergency with the birthing. My sister could do no better, and I have always wanted to have a big brother. Right now, Father is lying down for a nap, but soon he will be up and in the middle room. That will be your chance, but don't you think you ought to speak to my sister first?"

Laughing, he said, "My eyes have already spoken," and with that he tussled Jacob's hair and headed back toward the cottage.

Later that evening when all were together, Rabbi Ezar poured a glass of wine and sat it before Phoebe. If she accepts the offering and drinks this wine from the family's gold goblet, she will then be engaged to Tanner. The young couple looked at each other, and in silence their eyes spoke volumes. Phoebe picked up the goblet and drank it; not one drop was left. Grinning, we all began to congratulate the couple. At that point, Rabbi got serious, and by waving his hand, he asked us all to sit down again and be quiet.

What now, thought Lesia *imagining* herself drinking a goblet of wine just offered to her by Mara Chin with Andrew looking across the table to her, waiting to see what she would do. Rabbi Ezar then pulled out a small tin, opening it and removing a cloth wrapped around an item that was inside. He held it up for all to see and then began to tell the story Andrew had related to him. The story began on the Jordan River where John the Baptist was preaching and baptizing sinners when suddenly Jesus appeared and asked to be baptized too. John refused at first, but then Jesus said that John must baptize him in fulfillment of scripture. When Jesus arose from the water a Dove landed upon his shoulder and a voice from heaven spoke these words, "This is my beloved Son in whom I am well pleased." Jesus immediately left the scene and headed into the desert.

Andrew said he heard others say they heard thunder, but Andrew saw the Dove (the Holy Spirit), and he then began to tell the others, especially Simon, that Jesus was really the Messiah. Yet, as with all sinners, doubt and unbelief robs them of growing in the knowledge of God, therefore pushing aside the chance to accept the Good News when first heard. However, God is a God of second chances and is faithful to keep calling us. We should rebound from our sinful way, leaving the master of sin and accepting the giving ourselves to Jesus and serving Him, but some are stiff-necked and stubborn, which results in self-destruction, and many never change, therefore damning their souls.

Rabbi Ezar continued, "Andrew was patient with me and my ways, and as was said before, he became a son that was dearly loved. So, using metal that I had saved for a special occasion, I fashioned this item to give to him when we would next meet. Lesia, when you told us that you saw Andrew and gave him a kiss, my heart wept. This keepsake now should belong to you for you can see that it is a combination of his two loves." Unfolding the cloth, everyone sat spellbound, leaning forward to see what it was. He held up a piece of jewelry fashioned as a dove holding an olive leaf with the initial *L* between its feet.

Rabbi Ezar suddenly left the room since the emotional level was once again elevated as it had been for the last four days. Yet he knew he would express tears of joy when he would later kneel by the old, formerly wet shirt that seemed to never lose its color or age, given to him one day as they exchange gifts.

Lesia after calming herself ran to her sack and rummaged quickly for her locket, returning to show the locket and read the letter. Rabbi, who had returned, said, "Let me look at that. I can see that it is gold, and it seems to be a handcrafted piece." Looking at the back, he noticed something small like an initial or mark. Jacob offered to look at it to see if he could make it out. Then Tanner and the others soon agreed that the letter *T* was engraved on the back of the locket.

That could stand for almost anything, thought Lesia, but at least it narrowed down the possibilities; however, she still did not know if it stood for a first or last name. Looking at the two pieces of jewelry, Phoebe suggested that the piece that would have been Andrew's would make a beautiful brooch that Lesia could wear on her shawls. It would be simple to convert it into a brooch; thereby making it a very nice piece of expensive jewelry, a beautiful piece for a beautiful lady, and everyone agreed.

After retiring for the night, Lesia tried to think of all the names she had heard or read about that began with the letter *T*. Finally, exhausted, she slept.

Tanner now moved with urgency, for he wanted to get back home to tell his mother of his forthcoming nuptials. He needed to convince her to move here to the center of Ukraine to be with him and his wife-to-be. He also would have to decide on what to do with his small fur business and the small cottage. He needed to arrange for housing here, so he went to Rabbi Ezar, who gave him advice as to where to look for suitable land. There was land available that was free for the taking if the settler would live upon the land for a year and did not interfere with other rights to water or travel.

Phoebe was so impressed by this gesture because she was ready to leave her family and go with him wherever he lived. He hugged her to himself and said, "My wonderful wife-to-be. You are too precious to be lifted out of your wonderful family. My place is to become part of your family."

Tanner and Phoebe talked about their future together when Phoebe announced, "Well, my kind, wonderful husband-to-be, I have many sewing tasks that need to be started while waiting on a house. I will begin to make many beautiful rugs and clothes while you are gone." Hand in hand, they entered the cottage, and Tanner announced what his plans were. Tomorrow he would continue the journey to take Lesia somewhere. This now was the big problem now facing him, as well as her. Where? If miracles do occur, it was time for another one soon. The goodbyes were made, but it was decided that Old Grey would not go farther as she appeared to be a little lame in her right leg. "So, little donkey, you will be the lone beast of burden that must carry all the things," Tanner said. Yet, the trip appeared to materialize so easily for some reason. She pup was now called Mischief. Jacob had named her. Mischief had now grown a few more inches and seemed ready for the trip, as well.

Fine, thought Tanner, and as they waved goodbye, he prayed a prayer under his breath, "God, as a new believer, look over my wife to be and her family, and please God, prepare my mother to agree."

—m—

Tanner's home was in Luts'k, a town located much farther to the west than what he firmly believed to be the area of Lesia's origins. Where will the separation occur for Lesia was going through his mind but if that doesn't happen and she doesn't turn toward the East, he will just take her home with him. In addition, he wondered what the donkey's role was, an animal who appeared and then disappeared and who seemed to have heavenly guidance according to Lesia. She called it a God-sky, but he thought it was just spooky.

First though Tanner planned to pass through the hot springs area. He wanted Lesia see them and knew by then that their legs would benefit from the refreshing heat and curing the springs does for the whole body. For now, though that surprise would be on hold. Sleeping again under the skies illuminated by multiples of shining stars, Lesia wondered how many times Andrew lay awake with thoughts of His God making all of them. As Rabbi taught, "God hung each one and gave them a name." Wow, and again she was grateful for Tanner and Ahava as she emptied the old odd pan and wiped it dry to repack it tomorrow morning.

A week passed by, and Lesia noticed that Ahava was calm and not acting differently.

She mentioned this to Tanner and suggested that she could keep going until an intervention from the heavens happened. Under her breath, she pleaded, "Andrew, this was your country. God answered your prayers and gave you guidance. God, I need guidance for my journey, as well."

Tanner turned toward a path off the beaten trail, toward the big river. As they came into the thicker trees and out of the them, Lesia exclaimed, "Oh, the river is on fire." Steam was rising high and mixing with the breezes, and the sun was high overhead, making quite a picture with the glare emanating off the steam and the backlash waves over the river. But as she looked, she became aware that it was not the river itself, but a smaller body of water to the side of the river. Rocks surrounded the steaming water, interspersed with many paths leading down to that area. The grassy hillside was just right for a campsite and looked like it was frequently used in that fashion.

Tanner explained that this was a natural sight and many would come from far and wide just to stay a couple of days. People believed the mineral water had healing powers, so they would bring their sick ones to these healing shores. Some came as a family group, which made it safer for traveling. Others then discovered the open lands roundabout and decided to move stock and family to be closer thus able to come enjoy the comfort of the springs more often.

Tanner removed the load from Ahava, while Mischief headed down to explore what the odd smoking phenomenon was all about. "Careful," yelled Tanner, who again decided to control she pup with his belt. Tanner explained to Lesia, "Mischief won't like the water as it is very warm. Some areas, where the water is coming up from underneath the mountains, are even very hot."

Being careful not to fall on the rocks, they found a shallow area where they could wade up to their shoulders and necks. "Aah." What a great feeling came over them after walking so long and shuffling supplies from shoulder to shoulder. Lesia uttered thank you several times to Tanner for stopping and showing her this place, and of course she mentioned that Andrew stopped here. "I just know he did, Tanner."

Tanner would just shake his head then wondered why he had not met this man in passing on his journeys. No doubt they had passed in the twilight of time. But then again, he may have tuned out hearsay and news, for his loss of Junia had made him angry and aloof, not going to areas where crowds were assembling.

Tanner dipped himself completely under the water for a split second so that the heat even massaged his scalp and hair. He showed Lesia how they could take a sip of the water for the innards, but because of the sulfur smell, Lesia refused. "No thanks, she exclaimed, "but as for my feet, they love it."

"Well, let us be on our way." Looking around in exasperation, he questioned, "Now where did your donkey go?"

"Oh, no," Lesia cried out. She shook her dress as she ran up hill to see if Ahava was being led again to do the mysterious.

Yes, Ahava had seen the angel and had started to follow when He disappeared. So, she knew that something was to happen soon, but not just yet, so she turned around and came back to the clearing. When Lesia spotted her, in relief she remarked, "Ahava, you scared us again, so for now you will be wearing your halter so we can keep you close."

About two miles down the road, Ahava saw the angel again. He was standing on a much-worn large road path, which led to several small villages and she now knew it would lead to home.

Tkach Household

Meanwhile back at a little farm several miles west of town, for weeks as Nadia and Bohndan Tkach placed food and water out for the donkeys, they noticed that the animals were very quiet, not like themselves. They even were balky and temperamental. The Tkachs wondered what was going on, each trying to solve the puzzle. Placing food out and having very little eaten, the Tkachs became upset and temperamental themselves.

After several weeks, the animals began to act more normally; however, Ahava was still missing. Thinking back, Nadia realized that this strange behavior with all the animals began when Ahava herself left food untouched several days before she left, and then the rest of the animals followed her example later. Nadia was not aware of Andrews's plight at the time or of the coming weeks of gloomy depression that fell over the hill country from Ukraine to the western side of Patras as result of his death. When she learned of it, however, she began to suspect that Ahava knew of this event and somehow had expressed this to all the other animals. This was such an extraordinary concept that Nadia and Bohndan could hardly talk about it. Hearing Andrew talk about Malka was one thing but having this strange behavior now in their own barn and witnessing strange things themselves, things which go against the norm in the animal kingdom, was indeed a lot to process in the human mind.

The Tkachs themselves were not experienced in the supernatural, but they could not deny the real facts that all the animals had been off their feed for a week. One animal may get sick and go off its food, but the whole barn was so unusual that even the chickens were not laying eggs. This strange behavior affecting all the animals was farfetched, but maybe because of the Malka's lineage, it was a living possibility.

However, even though this strange behavior was happening, why it would make the little donkey leave the farm and not return after weeks of being gone? The Tkachs even left open the special gate just in case Ahava would return from her travels. They mentally would not even discuss the chance that she went somewhere and had gotten herself hurt or that a wolf had taken her.

Missing for days now just added to the puzzle. The Tkachs began to ask themselves if this event had something to do with Andrew, who had brought aging Malka and her offspring to the farm for special care. Andrew had mentioned that Malka had a gift that sometimes caused her to act strangely. Since Ahava was Malka's grandchild, Mrs. Tkach kept saying to herself, "It has to be the strange that is the source of all this nonsense." Often, she asked her husband, "Bohndan, do you think it is the strange?"

They wished now that they had asked more questions about the gift. "Maybe we should not have helped Andrew," Nadia whispered.

"Nadia, hush, woman. Don't be so afraid."

A year had gone by and some things had returned to normal but the unknown and unanswered questions seem never too far from both of their minds. Yet neither of them could bring themselves to lock the back gate, unaware of the influence of a strong, ethereal force upon them.

Tanner and Lesia were walking quietly now for they knew that soon Tanner must leave, heading westward toward his hometown. Yet Ahava had only made unusual a few miles back at the hot springs. Then Ahava jerked her head and stopped. The angel was on the path heading east. She turned and started toward the path when Lesia jerked on her halter causing her to stop. "Tanner, this is where we must part," Lesia said. Hugging him, she said, "If home is this way, we will not be so very far apart that you will not see me again, and who knows you may see me dancing at your wedding."

Laughing to keep the tears from flowing, he responded, "Wow, I never thought of that. If God truly is as great as He has been preached to us, we will see each other again. Didn't Rabbi say God gives us the desire of our hearts and watches over our footsteps, or was it He orders our footsteps?"

Lesia answered, "He has ordered our footsteps, and believe me, maybe He counted each one." On that note they again embraced, and Tanner watched for a few minutes as Ahava started a pretty good gait with Lesia beside her. He knew now that the donkey would play a major role in leading Lesia home. Someday he would hear the end of the story when he saw them again. Once again, he prayed, "Watch over these who have become precious to me and, please God, make my mother be understanding in this matter of moving."

※

When Tanner arrived home, it was late, so he just slipped quietly inside and headed for his room. The morning will be time enough to begin telling his mother his story.

In the morning Tanner awoke with great expectations and excitement for the first time in a long time. He had a renewed purpose for living, and that purpose was for loving. Phoebe had taken my breath away from the moment she smiled and said to me, "This is a blessing from the union of love," about the baby boy that we just delivered.

As Tanner entered the kitchen, he noticed the lethargic attitude his mother presented. Since his father passed away, his mother had lost all interest in the zest of life. He thought this move could mean a new beginning for her, as well, and decided that is where the discussion must start. "Mother, don't shake your head. We can do this and with extra help from the villagers that accept our *faith,* we can be more open and free. Look at your cloths, Mother. Your designs are so lovely. Oh, Mother, this will be a new beginning for you and for me." Shaking her head again, but this time as she wiped her tears, she picked up her zavolikannia scarves and hugged them to her bosom, and her eyes said yes. Tanner asked her where he could find the small locked box that held his father's important papers. She pointed toward the small cupboard above the others that made him start to get a higher chair to stand on but his mother pointed to another of his father's wood wonders a step-up box for her.

"Father, you were very tall and didn't forget about short people," he said as he hugged his mother, laughing. "Remember the makeshift ladder out in the barn used for you to help him hoist the straw upon the upper floor." Oh, Tanner, laughing now herself.

Reaching the locked box, he slowly returned his steps downward and recognized that a small hole was nicked on the corner of the box and surmised that a small mouse decided to taste the thing.

It was dusty and locked. What…where in the world would father had placed the key. Directing his mother to look among her things, he decided to check the work area where his father spent a lot of time making the wooden benches, tables, and knickknacks. He went toward the back of the little house to another shed, and lifting the latch bar he heard the old door creak, and became aware that lack of care and age were the only visitors lately. He had not even cared to come out and pick up the gifted trade that in his culture was handed down from generation to generation, especially to a beloved son.

Yes, Tanner had several gifts, and this will be utilized very soon to provide a home for his beloved Phoebe then maybe, soon after, a small baby crib. On that note, he jerked himself back to reality. The key, where will it be, here or there? He searched through several drawers and old bags, small tins and larger vases. Thinking the key was not to be found in the work area, he turned to leave, but excitement sprang forth as he spied keys hanging beside the door. Oh, wouldn't you guess, man—there hanging by the door. He quickly ran back toward the house, and with his mother watching over his shoulder, he tried each key.

Finally, one clicked, and the box opened. The papers now had the yellowish tint of age. A small decorative string separated groups of papers according to their importance. Tanner laid each bundle out on the table and picked up the newer ones, which read, "Deed ROMAN XXIV to the property of the Girogos Cohen Family. This day accepted is the silver (denarius) worth 16 bronze coins and 1 gold coin (aureus) worth 40 silver coins) that was placed on 1.183676 arpents one acre to be used for living rights. The whole acreage was a beauty and blessed place for the Cohens.

Next Tanner found a letter from the Roman Council that had agreed for families to travel out of upper Greece and migrate toward the north. He then saw his mother's full name. Giorgos Cohen and Catherine Ann Tkach would be owners of said territory and should file with the council again in that area.

Tanner ran his finger over this mother's maiden name, especially the letter *T*. "Would it be possible that Lesia is my cousin?" he wondered. "Would that be the answer to why a donkey woke me up one night, standing over me in the middle of my camp site? Could it be that God used me to help my own kin?" He sat down suddenly, his hands beginning to shake as the overwhelming comprehension of God's love began to flow through him. His mother clasped her hand over her mouth, thinking that her son just had a strange attack of some sort. She wondered why there was such a look of pain or is it amazement on his face.

Tanner with great joy explained to his mother the story of a man called Jesus. She then shook her head no when he mentions a baby in Bethlehem. No, babe, only the King—only our king. Then he explained to her about Lesia and a Rabbi who met Andrew and that Andrew was an eyewitness to all this way over in Jerusalem. He explained how the donkey also was gifted, and on that note, she stood up and remarked, "Time for tea and food. This is too much thinking for my head. Time to eat, son," and she headed off toward the kitchen.

"Yes, time to eat," he remarked. He was fearful that it would be hard for her to absorb all of this at her age when even he had trouble with it, and he was in the middle of the whole story.

Later that night, he stepped outside to look up into the sky, observing all the stars twinkling. He said a goodnight to his betrothed and in wonderment, "Lesia, if your last name is Tkach, then my mother is your sister!"

"God is so good," hummed Tanner as he prepared for packing and pitching. He went to his neighbor and asked if he could buy an ox, an oxcart, and two horses. The cart would hold the better things, and he would be able to pack one horse with additional items, while his mother could ride the other one. He relayed to Alex Kostas the good news of encountering the woman of his dreams and his decision to move close to her parents. Alex then asked what he was going to do about the property. "We haven't thought that far yet, but are you interested in buying it?"

"Yes, I am interested, so when you decide, please let us know what you want for it. I know your father had some nice furniture he was working on and I would be interested in looking at that also as I am an excellent farmer, but a mediocre carpenter."

As Tanner and his mother began to make decisions concerning the furniture, Tanner told his mother to set aside her favorite pieces for transport but suggested leaving the very extra-large table with ten chairs. He found a settee in the workshop that he thought Alex may accept that as payment for the ox and horses. Reminding his mother that his hands had helped father in the past, he was sure that the wood gift was still alive and well inside his head should his new wife or you want something, smiling.

Tomorrow with three neighbors for surety they will witness the sale signing of that former piece of paper from Rome to a Greek couple. Now seeing that things were moving faster than he had expected it was time to slow down. He needed to reassure his mother on all the other things-that she had come to love and to cherish. Tomorrow is another day, and on that note, he ordered his mother to rest, telling her that he would rise early and make breakfast for her. He blew out the candles then saw an old toy that his former Asher had played with. He picked it up, and seeing it still had some worth, he called Mischief his new little one to him. He watched as the pup began to bite and bark and finally pounce on the coon and squirrel tails with dried teeth from the wild boar intertwined in tough cow hide leather. Once again, the challenge was met and the toy was conquered.

The day of new beginning arrived at last, and Tanner and his mother left the old place behind to forge ahead into the new dream. On the way, Tanner told his mother more of Andrew's eyewitness account as told to Phoebe's father. "Andrew was in Jerusalem in the upper room on Passover eve when Jesus took bread and broke it, saying the bread represented His body that will be broken for them. He also took the wine, saying that it represented the new covenant that would be initiated when He shed His blood on the cross for the redemption of man. He did this so all believers would remember."

Then Tanner used the illustration of seeing a white wolf. Many scoffed and said that white wolves had never ever been seen in these parts, but we believed because we saw with our own eyes. In fact, that is when I wanted a wolf as a pet. "So, Andrew saw with his own eyes and that is why he could tell about the events surrounding Jesus. Then Lesia saw Andrew die for the gospel and that produced a very strong conviction for her." Tanner firmly believed that by the time they arrived in Kirovohrad his mother will have become a strong believer and that Phoebe will adore her.

Ahava

Seven miles down the road, Ahava saw the angel by a little clearing, so she pulled to the side of the road to head for that area. She knew Lesia needed to rest, and Lesia was glad for the stop. She gave Ahava some water before preparing some food for herself: a little water and a piece of cheese. While resting, Lesia spotted several wild carrots growing nearby. She and Ahava enjoyed their luscious nourishment.

Ahava began thinking about Mischief. The little one was growing in everyone's heart. But someday she would become a full-grown wolf. Ahava then wondered if she would still like them or if they would all become afraid of her. When she looked up she saw that the angel had veered off to the narrow path to the left of the main route into Zhytomyr. Ahava shook her head up and down and brayed. She then noticed the pouch on the ground, the pouch containing Andrew's sandals. She quickly bent over and picked it up and began rapidly trotting toward the path taken by the angel.

Startled, Lesia now with adrenaline flowing, began running to catch up with that frustrating animal, yelling as she began losing ground, "Come back here! I said come back here, Ahava. You have Andrew's sandals. No, Ahava. You can't take them and disappear again."

Ahava with the knowledge of all animals could sense a storm brewing and knew that they must quicken the pace and head toward, the farm where she and Grandmother Malka were nourished and taken care of by a loving and generous family.

Looking back at Lesia, Ahava feared that now she was going to faint at any moment and being out in deluge with Lesia on the ground was an unpleasant, disturbing thought. The sky began darkening and the sudden rubble of thunder caused Ahava to jump. Coming upon a pasture, she noticed that the sheep were huddled together, trembling, and baaing. Things were getting serious and Ahava longed for the peace and quiet of her familiar barn.

Ahava slowed down and turned just in time to see Lesia twist her ankle and tumble forward, striking her head on a rock that was lying beside the path. *Now what!* she thought. The clouds were going to open soon and safety would not be found standing here in the middle of the dirt road.

The sandals! Ahava trotted back with the bag still in her mouth and stood over Lesia. She let them fall near Lesia's hair and immediately a soft glow swept over Lesia's face and body. Lesia sat up and looked right into Ahava's eyes. "Ahava, what just happen here?" Ahava knew that no one would believe this, except Ahava could see the physical sign of a bump was on Lesia's forehead. Ahava neighed and bent down on her knees, letting Lesia know that she was to get on her back. Lesia too became more aware and could now see the clouds and increase in far-off lightning streaks and knew that rain was imminent.

Lesia buried her face into Ahava's neck, feeling the comfort of her warm body. Ahava began her quick trot-steps, going a little faster than she should be with such a special cargo on her back. They both knew that those sandals were not just bounded pieces of leather, and each meditated on the reasons for them to be together and to be the carriers of an anointed pair of Roman sandals. They both knew that this was God-ordained sky mission.

Ahava realized that she could take a shortcut across the pasture and headed for the barn, not the house. The barn was a better shelter from the storm, and Lesia needed to get some rest, for she was indeed falling asleep on Ahava's back. Ahava trotted up to the gate and with her nose butted it open enough to slip inside, going into the barn and heading for the stack of fresh piled straw. She tenderly knelt her right leg, and slowly, Lesia now asleep, fell gently sideways and was like a little lamb herself in the warm straw. The lighting now flashed and all the sky let loose its fury, like tears crying for a dead man who died on a demoralizing cross.

Lesia with the sandals clutched in her hand, slept far into the morning light. She never heard the raging storm nor the thunder that crashed outside the barn all night long but was sweetly dreaming of her time in Jerusalem when a darling fisherman came to the door to sell fish from the Sea of Galilee to the palace cook Mara Chin, and love was born in her heart while she was so young.

⁓ɯ⁓

Nadia Up at the Farmhouse

Rising later than her usual time because the storm had disturbed her night's rest, Nadia slowly went downstairs to the kitchen to begin some preparation for a hearty breakfast. Sometimes she felt too dejected to cook, but this morning was *different*, different in that the sun was beginning to shine and the birds and wind and the air all together were swirling in a special freshness. The aroma of the tea, and the kovbasa and eggs along with her special biscuits was excellent to say the least. She even sang her little tune while stirring the gravy, which mixed together smoothly like a sauce from heaven itself.

She had also started her favorite borsch for their supper. The beets washed and the cabbage cut just the right size added color to her faithful old soup pot.

Now she began thinking about when to add the rest of ingredients: the potatoes and then the tomatoes. She turned once more her kovbasa[17], browning nicely in the old, iron skillet of her mother's. Thoughts racing through her mind, "I need to get my pampushki ready. What is soup without bread?" and she moved the flour jar closer to the small stand. "Now where is my minced garlic?"

The aroma, wafting from the fragrance-laden kitchen, filled the upper floor. Bohndan began smelling the delightful odor, causing him to dress faster than usual and head downstairs straight for the kitchen to see if his stomach would find as much pleasure in the eating as his nose had pleasure in the sniffing.

Seeing his busy wife, he proceeded to set the table. Yes, he even pulled her apron strings loose as he passed by with two of everything in hand. You would have thought that this was a birthday or a special holiday by the way she was double tasking the food. He, being puzzled, just passed it off.

The animals also awoke with bountiful appetites; the chickens were squawking and the rooster crowing could have awakened the dead. The cacophony of sound also awakened Lesia, who sitting up still with

---

[17] Ukraine, Kielbasa-Poland

sleepy eyes was startled to say the least. She then laughed as she thought, *So this is what the farmer's life would be for her if she had been born into a farmer's family. Working in the palace was surely a far cry from this little scene.* She looked around the rustic barn and, seeing open holes here and there, knew that this was not the rich palace of a king, but a farmer's barn: cozy and warm with the smell of good, clean hay. It showed that this little barn got extra special attention even though over the years it had withstood the abuse of the weather. Looking for Ahava, Lesia noticed that the smaller door was open and sure enough Ahava was already enjoying the outside and braying to herself. As if that rooster wasn't making enough noise, now Ahava's sounds were mixed in.

Then through the hole above, Lesia saw the small wrens that had begun to sing their song for the day. "What is this all about? Well, now wait a minute. I am in a barn and with animals. I am not used to these circumstances. My life until recently was filled with the shouting of orders from Herodias or one of the other servants of greater authority than me. Well for now, this is all right because I am free, no longer a slave for life," and on that thought she spun herself around and touched her earlobes. Then with great enthusiasm, she yelled out loud, scaring herself, "I am free. I am free, free at last. Her vocalization mixed together with all this burst of energy in the barnyard, this energy expressing joy from animal and man alike filled not only the barn, but also the whole village.

She realized that Andrew's sandals were still lying on the straw and that she had slept with them. Is this the reason for my excitement this morning?

"Well, my sweet busy wife, listen, honey, it sounds like the whole barnyard is in a fine way this morning."

Bohndan shoved himself away from the table with a full stomach and a merry heart. Now to go see to the animals. Usually he would have done this first then come back into the house to have his own breakfast, but Nadia caused a different arrangement for this morning just by her enthusiastic cooking and eating cold food was not to his liking. So, eating a good farmer's breakfast came first. Whistling as he walked down the path toward the rustic old barn, he swung the milk bucket in step with his swaggered walk. Lesia heard the whistling and, not knowing who or what this might be, decided to find a neat little hideaway in the far-left corner among the hay. The corner did not have as much light this early in the morning, so she quietly squatted as close to the floor as possible and placed her back toward the wall. She held her breath as a middle-aged, whistling man swinging a bucket opened the big barn doors.

Daylight streamed throughout the barn. Lesia realized that her bundle was still lying in the bed of hay where she had spent the night. "Will he notice?" she wondered. She kept very still.

Ahava, hearing Bohndan, too came back into the barn and guess where she headed for, the far-left corner near the hay. Bohndan, seeing the little donkey near the hay, remarked, "Well, little one, you finally came home. Nadia will be excited when she finds this out."

Bohndan kept talking to Ahava as if he thought she understood until the excitement of her return was overridden by the distress of her absence and then the scolding began. Soon a shaking scolding finger at her and a deepened and stronger voice expressed his anguish, "How could you put us through this worry? You have no clue little animal that we promised Andrew we would be faithful to take care of all the ones that would come down from the Malka's line.

Nadia hardly slept thinking that you might be dead somewhere or had gone off doing the strange, and we'd never see you again. You are like a wayward child, so enjoy the day because the back door will be locked at night."

"Why, why are you over at the hay? I guess you finally got hungry and decided this place wasn't so bad after all, huh. Come here, little one." Ahava did not respond to the command to come and just kept standing staring down at Lesia hidden behind the hay.

Lesia motioned to Ahava, trying to shoo her away, but Ahava stood her ground like a bird dog fixed on its prey. Bohndan realizing that little donkey was looking at something had grabbed a stick just in case a rat or a snake had crawled in to get out of last night's storm. Slowly approaching the area, he gasped, "A woman! Who are you? Where did you come from?"

Yes, Lesia with the help of Ahava was now exposed to the stranger, a middle-aged man staring down at her while she hid her face. Lesia's thoughts flew back to palace days when at any given moment she would feel the strikes of the small whip on her back and hands, the whip Herodias used to correct her for any reason right or wrong. She remembered the name, Old Hateful, the name given by Andrew one day while in Jerusalem. Lesia's slave earring maybe gone, but not all her fear made from years of training as a slave in the House of Herodias.

She would stay still, waiting for a sharp order with its spill of explicit words before the little whip sent her to the special servant room without food for a day or days. The gift that came afterwards, given out of false kindness then would just make her hurt even more. Instead of true regret for her actions, Herodias would with the appearance of anger throw a small piece of jewelry at Lesia, then gruffly state, "Please forgive me, and now press out my dress." A piece of jewelry would never replace kindness or love. Then she would act so caring by saying, "Oh, by the way, I will keep it safe for you." Glad I did grab that bag of hers, maybe those were the ones.

After moving to Rome, missing special people in her life such as Mara Chin back in Jerusalem, Lesia would draw on her inward strength that caused her sometimes a homesickness that was met by weeping alone and nightmare of thought of maybe she should run away … but then the message that Andrew told her about the wonderful love of the man called Jesus would surface and what he preached about a servant's position. Serve like you are serving God. This when it replays through her mind would add the grit she needed to endure and he that endured to the end will be saved.

Ahava sensing that Lesia was frozen with fear, turned and walked over to the place where Lesia had slept and picked up her possessions and the sandals. She then brought them back and dropped them at

Lesia's feet. Lesia felt a calmness over her when she grabbed at them and hugged them to her bosom. She raised her head and watch him go, whew-good, his attention is now away from her and she took a deep breath.

With Ahava walking in the brighter light to grab the bags for Lesia, this is what got Bohndan's attention. His mind pondered no way. He went to her and examined more seriously, he got a shock for his little donkey was bigger, two hands-can't be.

Bohndan attention now fully on Ahava in the brighter light, he gets a second shock for his little donkey is expecting!! He began hugging her; looking right into her beautiful eyes and then embraced her again. Sorry girl, for the scolding.

He knew that this was the answer to why his beloved little donkey had been off her food and then gone for months. A mission. He couldn't help himself so he again hug Ahava.

The stranger, the woman now had his full interest, he knew that he must show this woman that she was safe. Turning toward Lesia, who was sitting in absolute obedience, he smiled and extended his calloused, old farmer's hand toward her in a gesture of fellowship.

Her eyes had seen this yelling man demonstrate love toward Ahava; now looking into his kind eyes realized this man had recovered from his startled double surprise. She extended her hand to him; he helped her up from the floor.

She knew this hand gesture. It was reminiscent of when Mara Chin would lift her up and put her on his lap and say that it was going to be okay, okie dokie. On taking his hand, she knew that this was a very kind and gentle person. She straightened out her clothing and looked around the barn, making sure she had everything that was hers. Clutching her bundle closer, especially the sandals, she smiled and began to follow him.

The path to the house was much worn, and she knew that many, many times this man and his family must have made the trip to and from the barn. She could see that a rocker, quaint and old though it was, rocked in the wind on the left side of the little porch. Simplicity compared to the plush homes of the governors of Judea and Rome, and especially that of the eccentric Nero, who maintained an abundance of artistic structures around the palace grounds. In fact, over kill people would say about it behind his back.

Lesia's eye caught a glimpse of the old cat stretching and curling back upon the old, tattered rag rug near the swing. The flower pots were freshly potted and looked like they had just been watered quite well from the storm.

Ahava seeing her leave with his gentle farmer did what she wanted to do and that was to run again to the back small pasture and do her famous back roll. Yes, God's sky timing for me also feeling the kick of one to be born soon.

Nadia was surprised to see Bohndan come into the house with a young woman in front of him. "What is this?" she questioned with her eyes. He told her, "She was in the barn. Now, sit down dear because the prodigal donkey is also home." She didn't know which way to react, wanting to see the donkey or to hear about this woman. She decided to start with the woman's story first-anyway her food needed some more watching. She gestured for them to go into the kitchen where she began to reheat the breakfast food for the new visitor.

Seeing the food, Lesia smiled, letting the Tkachs know that she was grateful for it, and especially grateful for the hot tea. Smiling, she told the Tkachs, "I know you are wondering who I am. Let me introduce myself. I am Lesia Chin."

Lesia then began the story of her life in the palace with her father Mara Chin. She relayed what she could remember of her early life and then the discovery of her adoption. She told of her desire to locate her biological parents and siblings, thus her reason for now being in the area. In her excitement to tell her story, she did not think about the locket. She was anxious to ask about how Ahava was connected to their farm. Nadia wanted to hear more of Lesia's story; however, she also wanted to see Malka's grandchild with her own eyes.

Ahava, seeing them all coming toward the barn, gave a greeting bray that they all understood; this was a happy occasion, and for Ahava the mission was accomplished.

"Yes, Lesia, this is Eleni offspring of Andrew's donkey Malka," Nadia told her. Andrew kept Eleni and brought her and Malka back here. He then went on his ministry with Eleni. We didn't even name the young colt we just started calling her Strange. This of course was news to Lesia, "Strange," laughing well it was kind of that when she found me, and she would not go away. I loved her at first sight and so I called her Ahava, which means love, then much later when she did the different, you are right her behavior is strange, laughing now together.

Nadia and Bohndan began a story of their own, going way back to the wedding of Carol and Daniel Tkach.

This kept Lesia spellbound till way after the midnight when everyone agreed to retire for the night. Tomorrow they would continue. Showing Lesia to a back spare room, the Tkachs left Lesia to her slumbers. The old, stuffed, duck-down mattress was so comfortable that she quickly fell asleep.

Before Nadia and Bohndan succumbed to slumber themselves, they looked at each other and wished for a moment that Andrew was here to know that the gifts of the donkey were still operating. They wanted to know more of the time when Lesia was in Patras, Greece, when Andrew was crucified.

The next morning the three gathered around the breakfast table once more. Lesia continues to relate her story, beginning now to comprehend the reality of her situation. Finally, she asked the couple, "What is your last name?"

"Tkach," they answered in unison. "Why?" Astounding the Tkachs, Lesia darted out of the kitchen, but soon returned carrying her necklace and brooch along with the letter. Looking carefully at the etching, they agreed that the small initial could be a T, causing Bohndan to take a good look at Lesia.

Hastily, Bohndan then left the room, needing to gather his thoughts. "This cannot be a coincidence. Lesia has the coloring and height of my oldest sister," he thought to himself. Catherine had taken care of him after their mother had passed on. She once mentioned a baby sister, but he never questioned, thinking the baby must have also died. He later met Nadia, settled down, and built the small farm while Catherine had met Giorgos[18] Cohen and moved somewhere toward Greece. Bohndan never heard from her again, life moving on with or without news.

Thinking back over his life, Bohndan regretted the loss of a young daughter, but rejoiced in the life of his son Daniel. Daniel's marriage to Carol was the highlight of any parent's dream for their child. Life had its twists and turns, some ugly times and some kind; however, what greater joy could there be than a sister once lost being returned to the lineage.

Andrew had blessed Daniel and Carol and told them that they too would have a son. As these words of Andrew had now come to pass, would Andrews's words in Bohndan's dream last night also now be coming true? Andrew had said that there would be an amazing surprise that would come from out of the south and would connect the hearts of many. After awaking in the night, Bohndan had pondered this dream for a while but had almost forgotten it by morning. However, he noted that Lesia is a surprise,

---

[18] Greek spelling.

she has a T on her necklace, and she comes from the south. He still didn't know the meaning of the final statement, "Would connect the hearts of many." What is the end? Bohndan tried to remember if Catherine ever had a necklace, but alas she is not here and for all he knew could be dead.

Taking the ring, Bohndan returned to the kitchen; his breathing ragged and his heart beating rapidly. He laid the ring beside the necklace. They both had the same quality and color of real gold, a matching set, lying side by side on the table as three people pondered the scene. "Now let's see if my ring has the same etching," Bohndan said, his hand now shaking as he turned to look inside the ring. He could not now withhold his thoughts, "The same hands that had made this ring had made the necklace, my loving, late father."

"Your father, Lesia," he said with quivering lips. "You, you are my baby sister. Look for yourself. Both etchings match. My sister gave me this ring because it belonged to our father."

Lesia dropped to her knees and with her head in her hands wept as one who had lost and then found a piece of her heart. Soon Bohndan and Nadia went to their knees and embraced a woman who had stepped from a lost past into the present day.

When control of their emotions returned bringing them back from shock to reality, they all praised God. Nadia for the first time felt a change in her soul from unbelief to the wondrous reality of the workings of Almighty God. To quote Andrew, "Nothing is impossible with God and to those who trust Him."

As several months passed, Lesia became part of the family routine. Bohndan and Nadia watched her become a good farmer. She also had become a skilled rider. She could gather eggs and bake a cake to perfection. Nadia, now with help inside and out, was so pleased, sometimes pondering what it would have been like if only her baby girl had lived.

Ahava was soon to become a mother, another baby joining Malka's line. Bohndan kept a close eye on her as the moon waxed toward fullness because many animals delivered during a full moon. Lisa and the Tkachs discussed names one night over supper. They felt that Ahava's gift would continue, perhaps with the foal leaving for another country, bringing the gospel message and healing to areas far beyond them.

Exhausted by the possibilities, Lesia remarked that she couldn't think of another name.

She also didn't know who the father was, yet she remembered that Ahava had left for a while, not reconnecting with her until she had reached the mouth of the Tyras River. Bohndan laughed. "Maybe, we will call it Wandering Star." Little did Bohndan know that the new foal would have a mark on its forehead. Soon the braying of another donkey could be heard, a nice-sized boy. On the night of delivery, Ahava again saw the angel. She recognized that this would be the end of her reign and the beginning of another. The gifts go on. Winter settled in, and Lesia learned many new things: building fires, cutting wood, candle making, drying meat, and canning. The northern climate required heavy coats and warm boots. Some days were enjoyed by taking a sleigh ride and visiting a close neighbor. During times of severe cold, warming pots helped revive cold hands and toes. Andrew's sandal still had the power to heal. When winter weather brought with it the common cold, Lesia then put the sandal to her head.

—ɯ—

Tanner and his mother enjoyed the final days of summer. By fall, Tanner had made good progress on the new house. Phoebe of course was a great help as she seemed to be so gifted. They were also blessed to have met some supportive neighbors who willing gave of their time and effort toward the project. Rabbi's skill with stone and wood added greatly to the design and style of the new house. Tanner thought, "Yes, my father's gift is alive and well in my hands, too," and soon the thoughts of long weeks and months of fur trapping began slowly slipping away as his woodworking skills increased and thoughts of his sweet Phoebe being left alone were too much to bear. Mischief was becoming aggressive, and Tanner thought that she would soon run off and join a pack. Although some wolves do stay tame, Mischief is what Jacob called her, wasn't giving that indication.

He knew that soon he would be without a pet once more.

All the family wondered about Lesia and prayed the best for her. They knew that Ahava was an integral part of Lesia's mission and really wanted to hear how things turned out, hoping that one day Lesia would return to the area.

Jacob was turning into a fine young man and was interested in studying in Egypt. His mother and father encouraged him and yet hated to think that he soon would be on his own.

Having two wonderful women, Phoebe and his mother, together in his life, Tanner felt blessed. Both women were adept at sewing, cooking, and many other skills that when Tanner pulled a muscle in his back, his women had the expertise to medically minister to him with poultices and herbs, causing him to raise from his bed of pain in short order.

Soon winter would arrive so preparations began in earnest. Tanner noted the thickness of the cornstalks and knew that this winter was going to be a bad one. The men spent time killing and skinning animals, while the women dried the meat and made candles. Tanner and Jacob began cutting their winter's supply of wood. Jacob liked showing off his strong arms, trying to outdo his soon to be brother-in-law. Tanner thought, *Well, little younger brother-to-be, never fool with an expert*, and the chopping war began. Youth had no chance. Experience won the day.

Rabbi Ezar used his metal-working skill to outfit Phoebe's new kitchen with cooking utensils. In addition, he constructed a beautiful brazier oven incorporating various sized stones for beauty and utility. He added a large flat stone on the side as a warming area for prepared food.

The windows were framed with strong, wide lattice, making strong shutters. After this, Tanner began to work on the new table and chairs. He somewhat regretted leaving the old one back at the homestead. *It would have been great*, he thought, sighing because it would take some hard sanding and hours of work to get the details in the backs of the chairs. He was glad for father's old tool box.

The Sabbath was an important day for Rabbi Ezar and his family, so became important for Tanner and his mother, as well. Beginning at sundown on Friday evening, the Sabbath ritual began. It was so good to relax; however, sometimes on a moonlit night, Tanner along with Mischief would slip out to find some deer meat. One night, Mischief began snarling, her hair rising upon her back. Tanner took one arrow out ready to shoot when a big white wolf appeared over by the clearing. The wolf howled the love call of the wild, and Mischief stood for a few moments of indecision. She circled Tanner a couple of times when again the white wolf howled his command. Mischief left Tanner, but he accepted the inevitable since it was the *white* wolf, the legend of mystery, that had made him love wolves in the first place.

As Tanner told the story at breakfast, he said, "Now, white wolf has taken my Mischief."

"Supposed to be," said Phoebe over her morning cup of tea. She reminded Tanner not to mention this to her father. Without saying, he was not to mention a stolen kiss or two either as he quickly skinned and gutted the deer and hung it from a wooden beam in the snow bin outside. "Now that some good deer meat is prepared let the snows begin," he mused. He never thought he would ever be happy again after pneumonia had taken Junia his first love. He was thankful for the part that Ahava played in the finding of Lesia, which led them to Rabbi and Phoebe. He wondered if Andrew were alive what stories he could tell that would seem as impossible and unreal as this one.

Springtime seemed to burst forth on the hillsides, along the rivers and into the villages. People were gathering up for loads of sellable items and organizing groups to caravan to the mouth of the big river where ships with great sails would be coming up the Black Sea. Yes, spring is the time of year when a man's fancy turns again to love and soon his coming marriage.

Jacob pointed out again that on one of the trips down the river, he would board a ship that would be setting sail toward the Aegean Sea and south again toward Egypt. Everyone was saddened by that announcement but kept their remarks to themselves.

Springtime preparations were also occurring on the Bohndan farm. Bohndan and Nadia began thinking about taking some of the sheep and three oxen to sell. In great anticipation, Lesia exclaimed, "You could also sell some of the beautifully crafted clothing you made during the winter." Lesia also suggested that they travel west first and then turn south so that they could stop at the springs where she and Tanner visited on their way north. "We could also visit the family where I met Phoebe and her father. That would give us a chance to rest awhile before heading on to the mouth of the Tyras." Yes, there was much talk and excitement was high. Little did they know the destiny that was before them.

Over the long winter months on several occasions, Lesia would handle her necklace and brooch. "Andrew, you saw the dove sitting on Jesus's shoulder. Oh, my love it seems so long ago since I last saw you, yet not so long if I don't count the days. Loneliness makes it seem like an eon. The *L* and the olive leaf were so delicate and now so special, representing the bonding between soul mates. He that endures to the end shall be saved," she whispered as she replaced the pieces back into the drawer. The mystery of the *T* on her necklace was now solved. She now knew where she belonged and was committed to becoming a strong Tkach so help her.

Lesia had finally mastered the art of milking but not without several overturned buckets and a few tails brushing her babushka moments. Killing the snake, however, took top honors along with the best screaming she could master. "Earth worms now seemed mild in comparison." She smiled. She contemplated the forthcoming travel arrangements, thinking that traveling with a donkey was one thing, but now with several sheep and three oxen? "Well, anything is possible, and if my brother can do it, so shall the newest member of the clan."

May brought an abundance of sunshine and various shades of green, spreading across the landscape from the hillsides to the low-lands. Bohndan worked at selecting the sheep and other animals for the trip to the sea. He had to borrow Bo'bik a sheepdog from a Roman neighbor since his faithful friend of many years had died over the winter. Lesia and Nadia helped load the carts with crafts, candles, and the special Ukrainian colored eggs nicely packaged to be sold at the dock or put on ships for other ports. Buyers and sellers would exchange goods, sharing their special talents, all obtaining needed merchandise for the coming year. One year, Nadia found a large, good quality cooking pot and was quite pleased with it. She hoped that this group of travelers would be at the dock again this year.

A special joy at these occasions was listening to those with musical talents. Participants usually ended up joining in dancing and singing the songs of the Black Sea culture. Some years there were even performances by clown acts.

Lesia remembered meeting Tanner there, noticing him while he was looking at knives and arrows. She wondered about him for a moment and commented to Nadia. "He sounds like a real outdoorsman, and to think he is going to marry this girl he just met," she observed.

"Sounds like a lot to ponder on, Lesia."

Lesia also described the events surrounding the birth of the baby. "The woman's screams scared me thoroughly. I had never witnessed anything like that before. But the resulting bouncing baby boy was a joy to behold. Did I tell you that the parents named him Andrew because of the benefit they received from Andrews's sandal?"

"What did Andrew's sandal have to do with birthing?"

"Well, Christine was having a difficult delivery, so I laid the sandal on her stomach. It caused a miracle."

"Do you still have those sandals?"

"Yes, I have carried them with me since Patras."

"Do you believe this really happened, or did it just startle the woman?"

"No, Nadia, it was what you call 'the Strange,' but I have always called different the God-sky gift." Then Nadia knew what Lesia was talking about, knowing also that it defied explanation. She just shook her head in confirmation and returned to the packing the last cart. Lesia thought for a second and reminded herself to go and get those sandals. One just never knew what might lie ahead. Bohndan insisted that everyone get to bed early. "We'll rise early tomorrow morning and set out on our journey." He had agreed to take the route that Lesia said was miraculous and marvelous. Lesia tossed and turned for a while, but soon by placing the sandals with the God-sky gift on them beside her-sleep came, causing her to drift off to the unknown music of lands far away.

The next morning Ahava was edgy. She watched her colt frolicking in the yard, jumping, and turning. Little did the Tkachs know that Wandering Star had seen the angel, and that Ahava knew her little one was to leave with Bohndan. That was the problem because Bohndan did not have taking a little donkey on a journey on his to do list.

Bohndan finally noticed Ahava coming out from the pen area with her colt. Star stood as if to say, "Okay, ready to go." Ahava then saw the angel and watched as her colt walked over to the carts and stood beside one of the oxen. "Hey, you. No, you get back over to your mother. Ahava, what!"

Then together all spoke, "It is the strange." Nadia almost became unglued.

Lesia, thinking out loud, said to Bohndan, "Wandering Star is to go with us."

"Are we to sell him?" he asked.

"I don't think that is what we are to do, but if we are, how do you stop the plan of God?" Silence was the answer. They just watched to see what Wandering Star would do next. Finally, Bo'Bik broke the silence by barking at a wandering sheep, and the trip started out in earnest.

Lesia mention the rock as they passed by the pasture like field, the shortcut that Ahava took that led to the barn from the main road. "This shortcut is where my head and this rock met when my ankle turned while I was running after Ahava when she took the sandal bag." Lesia had them all laughing at the story of the event with the unpredictable donkey.

They finally stopped for the night. "I'm surprised at how obedient Wandering Star has been. He has given no signs of turning back," Bohndan commented.

Lesia pondered this, knowing that something would happen soon, but not knowing where or when. "Yes, Andrew, I wish you were here. You were always so sure and levelheaded." She remembered the way Andrew always gestured with his hands, emphasizing his point. Lesia wondered if she was supposed to go with the donkey; after all she did follow Ahava all the way from Greece, finally meeting her brother and his lovely wife. "Would there be more?" Some things the mind just must let it go for a little bit so one could deal in the now and let tomorrow take care of itself.

Soon enough, today's episode transpired. One contrary sheep began driving Bo'bik out of his mind. Bohndan finally tied it up, and everyone got some instant relief. Later that evening, they all settled down to a pleasant dinner. The air was still warm, and the evening glowworms lights couldn't be lovelier.

Wandering Star continued to be well-behaved and followed without any trouble, which the Tkachs found unbelievable since his mother was Ahava. They discussed the possibility of selling the colt to a stranger, wondering what the buyer's reaction would be to the strangeness of Wandering Star's ways. Everyone developed a mental picture that caused much head shaking.

Wandering Star seemed tuned in at times to what the group was discussing and would come over to beg for a carrot or apple. Sometimes Bohndan would take one bite out of his apple and then give the rest to the colt. "Why did you do that?" Lesia asked. Bohndan told her that he had started this practice with Malka and had kept it up with Ahava. "So, why not with Star?"

"Funny how we humans change our behavior for an animal, making them like one of our own children." They all agreed that was the case and laughed about it.

"It didn't matter the size or the species either," echoed Nadia. She recounted the story of one of the chickens that she could not have for dinner because it followed her all around the barnyard, even wanting to come into the house with her, but she did limit its access to the porch only.

The next two days brought them closer to where they would turn down the path off the main River Road and head toward the little village Kirovohrad* where Rabbi Ezar and his family lived. "It will be great to see them again," Lesia remarked, as she wondered about Tanner. That's when they were suddenly surprised when Star, who was walking ahead of them, without being told turned down the widen path Lesia was pointing out to Nadia.

"The Strange," Nadia whispered under her breath.

All went well as the group turned onto the well-worn path. Then Bo'bik herded the sheep and the oxen turned without any mishap, probably thinking they were coming to the end of their journey and the hard work of cart-pulling.

As the Tkachs approached the village, supper was in progress. Catherine and Dell, and Phoebe were just setting the table when they heard the rumble of sheep baaing and a dog barking. The women went outside to see what the commotion was about, thinking that a new family was moving into their area. "Oxen, hurray," yelled Jacob, "That is exactly what is needed for our family." Both Jacob and Tanner wondered if one would be for sale.

Coming up the lane behind the troupe was Lesia and Nadia. Lesia broke into a run and waved to Phoebe as she rounded one of the carts. The reunion was on with hugging all around and a cacophony of talking so that Rabbi, hearing the spectacle took, off toward the back room, thinking now what is it with these Gentiles.

If he had waited a minute, he would have known it was Lesia and would have joined in the fray. Catherine kept on watching the bread and stirring the soup, unaware that her brother was now standing outside and that soon her heart and soul would be blessed beyond measure.

Jacob and Tanner along with Bo'bik and Bohndan settled all the animals behind the house. Old Goat was ready to butt the dog, but when Star walked up to it and stared with compassionate eyes, Old Goat stopped and walked to his own area. Jacob was amazed that Old Goat seemed to like Lesia's donkey. Bohndan said, "Well, when Ahava was here, she was expecting. Wandering Star is her colt."

"No way." Everyone immediately had to touch and examine Star from tooth to tail. "Why did you bring him with you?" was the next question.

Lesia explained, "We didn't. Ahava pushed the colt toward us, and Star obeyed and without hesitancy he followed along."

"Wow! Do you think Ahava's colt has that God-sky gift you talked about? The same gift that Andrew's donkey had?" Phoebe inquired.

"Yes, but what we don't know is to whom he will be sold or if a sale will be made. It is a total mystery to us right now," Bohndan told her, shaking his head as they all headed toward the house for supper. Catherine, wishing to freshen herself because of the extra company, had already left to go to her bedroom. Finally, everyone entered the dining area and sat down when Catherine came in and stopped, mouth agape but without sound. She just ran over to Bohndan and began to weep. Rabbi wondered what was going on with Tanner's mother and feared that dinner would grow cold. Bohndan and Nadia together hugged Catherine and soon were weeping themselves. "We thought you might be dead. We did not hear from you. What happened?" So many questions all coming out at once and nobody answering or hearing the answers till finally a tap on a wine goblet silenced the cacophony.

Rabbi, in wisdom, pronounced, "From this, we can tell that one person who was lost has now been found. We shall now continue with the blessing of the food and then we shall listen to the miracle that if the truth is known will amaze us all." Quiet reigned for a moment and then the passing of the meal that tasted like it was made in heaven, for Catherine was quite an excellent cook, and the touch of her hands was on every dish and was much appreciated by Dell.

Tanner was in shock as the story progressed. "If Bohndan is my uncle, then Lesia is my aunt. The *T* mark on the necklace? Did that help?" he questioned.

The answer was yes, backed up by the ring that Bohndan was now wearing. "Catherine was the older sister and knew about the baby girl but we thought that we would never ever see that child so out of sight was out of mind and this helped the loss. Soon our lives went on separate of each other."

"How and when did you return to this area, and why didn't you try to find me?" was the bigger question that was on Bohndan's mind.

"My husband promised that as soon as we got settled, he would try to find you, but his illness interrupted things so that all our energy was used to eke out a living. Traveling was too hard for a woman alone. The years passed, and soon Tanner became of age so that he started his own fur business. By that time all the thought of looking for you was lost as my mind and my injury I became forgetful. But thanks to the mercy of the God above, my eyes have not only beheld my brother, but my baby sister, as well. This whole miracle was set up by the one promises our mother whispered before she passed on. 'He that holds the winds and clouds holds the destiny of every bird and knows the heart of all matter and, if so, His will be wonderful to his faithful children, for His virtue is love.'" Jacob was listening to this interchange. In the past, he had felt something was stirring inside him, thinking that it was just wanderlust, wanting to see what the outside world was like. He now knew it was that unseen calling, the calling that caused everyone to acclaim victory to the living God. Now his Torah learning was making some sense as the Jesus story began to be open to him in real life, his life with miracles that he has seen with his own eyes and testimonies that he has heard with his own ears. This story of Lesia's eyewitness account about Andrew. The remarkable events surrounding Tanner and Ahava were further proofs of God's-sky intertwining miracles in lives.

Jacob wanted this calling. He wanted to be like Father Abraham and set out for the country that God would show him. He might also find a lovely wife like Rebekah who watered Abraham's eldest servant's camels. His mind did not contemplate Andrew's end. He was only fixed upon Jesus, the Messiah, the King, and the knowledge that soon He would be reigning one day in Jerusalem. His Messiah was Jewish, and this was a very deep connection inside his soul.

Jacob started to blurt this information out, but he immediately stopped himself and closed his mouth. He knew to honor one's parents was a strong commandment. He recognized that first he must talk to his parents together and must do so alone. Yes, a blessing to a son was honor. He also considered according to custom Phoebe's betrothal and her wedding, he can't leave now.

Silently, Jacob picked up the dishes and removed them toward the kitchen. He began to place the pans on the fire for water to boil for the cleanup preparations, thinking to himself, "Yes, I need a woman that can cook also."

The candles were burning low before everyone decided to head for sleep. Tomorrow morning the excitement would begin again. Phoebe thought that tomorrow morning she would begin making wedding plans now that everyone was here, and then they could continue to the open market on the mouth of the river. She would approach her father tomorrow. Tonight, she leaned over and kissed her parents' good night.

The next morning both Jacob and Phoebe approached their father. Rabbi heard Jacob first, soon would be followed by Phoebe. Rabbi listened to Jacob and gave a wave of the hand that he had heard enough and would give the answer after midmorning prayers.

Jacob seemed pleased enough about his father's demeanor and went straight out to attend to the farm animals.

He noticed that Old Grey's leg was not looking very good this morning. He might have to change her workload.

Before breakfast, Lesia wanted to check on Wandering Star so went out to the barn. She saw Old Grey there and noticed that her leg was feeble and felt compassion for her. Wandering Star came over to stand beside the old horse, sniffing the wounded leg and soon the beginning of a small ear twitch occurred unnoticed by Lesia.

Meanwhile, Lesia turned and went to get Andrew's sandal, passing Jacob who was a man on a mission to get all the chores completed. Phoebe, Catherine and Dell were busy finishing the breakfast preparations with Nadia and Bohndan smiling and in good spirits themselves. Lesia put aside the errand she had for Old Grey and jumped right into helping the other women. After breakfast, Lesia helped with the clearing of the dishes and wiping the table before she left to go look for her bundle that held the sandals. Taking out the right one, she again held it to her face. The rose aroma still lingered there, and her heart felt such a wonderful peace. Lesia finally remember old Grey, she thought, *This must work even if it is for an old horse and with the sandal in hand headed down to the barn.* "Here, old girl. Yes, your eyes talk of your pain. Oh, Andrew, in the name of Yeshua may a miracle happen." She placed the sandal against Old Grey's leg, causing the horse to jerk and fall down.

Lesia screamed, and Jacob echoed with, "What in almighty frog legs. Lesia, did she just up and die?" Old Grey answered that question by getting up and taking off running, not quite like a new young stallion, but good enough that she would be granted a few more horse years

Phoebe was excited while talking to her father and said she would like to have a short ceremony, for she had not been down to the mouth of the river for a long time, and it would be like a small honeymoon. "Don't you agree, Father, that we could do this? For surely you know that we will be living just down the road soon. We can do something to celebrate with all the neighbors later." Rabbi sensed that maybe it was a sign. She would without knowing it would be accompanying her brother to see him off on his quest to find himself, and they might not behold his face for a long while until destiny returned him again.

Rabbi announced at the dinner table what the great events would be and then described the order. Pheobe's first then Jacob's. "First we must remember the marriage ceremony is two-part covenant. The first part, the *kiddushin*, has been completed. This ceremony connects the couple as two equals in a marriage covenant." We were very happy with the betrothal. They all laughed, remembering how quickly Phoebe drank down the wine, nary a drop left.

"Now the sacred bond, the *nissuin*, will take place. This ceremony connects the couple with God in a permanent relationship. Tanner tomorrow that home of yours will be inspected, so I'm just letting you know."

Tanner swallowed hard, left, and headed toward his homestead. Yes, he was working hard and one thing yet that was a special window made like from (faience-faenza) oh now father wish these ears of mine would have listened better when you explained some of the how and whys but will do the best on this or just place up boards for holding space and deal with it later. He had from hardwork some expectation of praise forthcoming about his wood working skills. The table, chairs, and special cabinets all had been lovingly carved and smoothed. Another feature was the iron hooks for holding the pans and pots. His mother's weaving and her pottery enhanced the home with great color. "Yes, my bride will be very pleased, and I will have great peace with my in-laws." He would have visions during his sleep of all that was to come. He was amazed of how some things came to be and his faith in God was increasing daily.

Tanner worked way into the night to put finishing touches to his new home, a home that soon would hear the footsteps of his own sons and daughters. "Yes, Mother, you will be a grandmother someday. You can count on it."

"The next announcement concerns Jacob who has asked for a blessing to go out into the wide world to find himself. With some of you going to the mouth of the river, I am giving him permission to go with you, and all of you must see that he has a clear voyage or a clear direction before you leave him. Mother, now please no tears." Dell quickly left the room to control her feelings. She knew that someday he must go out to seek his fortune but would not face it until now. "No," she cried, "he is still my baby." Jacob has had some adventurous dreams himself and not yet told anyone just because he too, was hesitant about leaving home.

Lesia knew now that Jacob was named after an old patriarch of the Jewish people. Andrew's sandals were going to be placed on a second Andrew, and Jacob would be worthy of them. Finally, she had to come to grips with herself to be able to part with them. They were such a part of Andrew. She didn't know what she would do now if she ran into any who were sick. "No," she chided herself, "a promise is a promise." She had given her word to the old couple when they asked, "Will you give these to someone?"

Jacob now heard the story of the sandals from Lesia, and he drank in every word. He told her of his secret, the music in his head and the visions of helping little children and elderly persons even those whom he would not understand their language.

Lesia acknowledges to herself, "No better person than one who hears the musical call, right Andrew."

He shook his head and could not believe he had confided to Lesia but maybe they both had plans that God was working on. They both did not see the angel smiling.

Jacob was a little skeptical, and yet God had let him see the miracle of healing on Old Grey's leg, as well as the miracle that occurred for Christine when her baby was about to be born breech.

Rabbi was taken aback when he saw the lovely cottage and all the love worked into its design even with an extra room, which showed that Tanner was planning on being a family man indeed. "Daughter, you have been blessed, and all of heaven is at your beck and call," was just one of Rabbi's blessings bestowed during the evening ceremony. "May your daughters be as Rachel and Leah," and on and on he went.

Jacob blessings included, "Ah, the smile of my son who is obedient, kind, and trustworthy, bringing honor to both your mother and me, considerate to your sister and compassionate with other people and animals. May God give you of heaven's dew and of earth's richness and abundance of grain and new wine. May your sons and daughters honor you, and may God help you find your high calling."

Lesia was overcome with the richness of real love that parents have for their children. Her thoughts went back to Huldah and all the children, especially the one from Rome, Alma Delores. She had in her heart and head now that starting a children's school was her calling, and since this endeavor was to take place in the area that Andrew had ministered, she wanted to call it Andrew's School[19]. She would have to go around and sign up children. Without any background, the work would be hard, but so was living with old Hateful. She chuckled to herself because from the past experiences came lots of insight and wisdom. "Dearest love, reach down from heaven and guide me into my calling. He that endures to the end will be saved could be the school's motto." She finally was alerted back from

____

[19] Later a church was named Saint Andrew

her inner meditations just in time to see two people kissing behind the kitchen door.

Lesia was so excited for Phoebe. Upon seeing this tender moment, she replayed a scene in her mind between herself and Andrew, thinking that it might not be right to do this since Andrew is now with God. But, nevertheless, she remembered many happy moments inside her flesh, and she knew that she was not dead yet.

Living without the sandals to sleep with would be a challenge even for the strong of heart. She pondered over the question, "Should she just let one sandal go with Jacob, or should he wear them both." Then she realized that Jacob must try them on. "Jacob," she called, "if you have a minute, quit eavesdropping on your sister."

He laughed and remarked, "Well, how will I know how to hold a sweet maiden when the time comes?"

"What happened to the high calling, sir?" she reminded him. Smiling, they both exited the house to go gather the eggs and feed the animals.

Bohndan and Nadia were enjoying meeting for the first time, the neighbors and had exchanged some of their goods for what they could use back on their farm. Bo'bik and the sheep were taken, but then they remembered that the dog belonged to their neighbor and that they promise to return him when they got back. One ox and cart was sold to a neighbor with friendship thrown in as an extra value. The young couple John and Christine came to supper one night and brought the baby boy whom they had named Andrew since the miracle of his sandal had healing for the birthing process. As they recounted the story again. Bohndan and Nadia were riveted to every word. Nadia leaned over and whispered to Bohndan, "Do you think it was the Strange?"

Smiling, he just reached over and gave her a sweet kiss. "Yes, and much more, darling."

To say who stole the show that night with his big eyes and drooling lips was a child that brought great joy to his parents and all who met him. Knowing his tenuous start in life gave appreciation that he would now have a chance to grow into adulthood.

Supper was again delightful, but soon the morrow would arrive, the day appointed for the journey. Knowing that Jacob would be traveling far away for an unknown length of time unfortunately brought a somber mood that followed them to bed.

Sunshine is great for the soul and the day looked promising as the troupe set out on their journey. Rabbi Ezar and Dell Rubin stood arm in arm as they watched the young ones and Lesia along with what remained to sell at the big community get together at the Black Sea.

They continued to watch until the group passed out of sight around the curve in the path that led to the main road that people began calling River Road. Rabbi Ezar looked toward heaven and said the Shema.

Catherine had desired to stay at Tanner's new home and thus was not present to see them off. She had hugged Tanner, her son the night before, having experienced his departure for extended lengths of time in the past when he would be gone for a week or two while running his fur routes. After she awakened, she walked around the house careful not to bother what she knew was Phoebe's. She was so happy inside that her son found such a wonderful woman to become his wife, her daughter-in-law. The new rocker was just fine, as well, so fine that she was soon snoring in a little, old lady fashion with her shawl tucked around her shoulders, unaware of the beautiful cat that was making its way around to observe just where it might have a short nap also.

Wandering Star picked up the pace and pranced up beside Lesia, acting like he knew that Lesia just parted with something very wonderful and valuable to her. She reached over and stroked him. Maybe it was just her own thinking, but that thought was so very clear when Star came beside her. "You, my sweet one, what are your plans?" talking to Star like he understood her. She was almost expecting an answer. Yet even knowing and believing in Yeshua, His realness and miraculous ways, was almost too much for one's brain to grasp. Maybe our thinking, that is why many people have not made a choice yet to serve the one true God, the One who created everything.

Lesia looked around her, noticing the beauty and wonder of God's blue sky, the greenery of varying shades in the earth beneath, the awesomeness and exquisiteness of the lovely wild flowers scattered around. She felt the coolness of the breeze blowing through the trees and gave thanks to the One who created it all.

Ahead of Lesia hand in hand walked the happy couple. Jacob was behind her, using his staff to direct the oxcart, accompanied by faithful Bo'bik acting like he was the one directing the oxen. "No, sheep." Lesia laughed. Bohndan and Nadia handled their ox and cart, which contained provisions for the journey. Passing by the hot springs, they decided not to stop and have any more delays, for they knew several days had already been lost. They were now concerned that maybe a big merchant ship had already come in and had now gone.

Huddled by the campfire Tanner had expertly fixed, they rested for the evening and ate some very tasty cheese along with the bean soup. Lesia rearranged her blankets close to Nadia and her brother. "To think that this is my family. I did not even know about them when coming up the River Road, and now as I am going back down the road, we are together. Go figure." With that thought in mind, she listened to a night call of an animal the white wolf and pulled her blanket more closely around her.

The journey went smoothly until one wheel on the oxcart cracked. Time was then lost as Tanner had to take some hours to fix it. Thank heavens for his carpenter skills and the judicious use of some grape vines tied into knots, which acted like bonding strings. Progress was slow going, but they were still able to continue. That was one problem solved. Another arose when the Bo'bik ran off. They called and called, however, were unsuccessful in bringing him back. "Maybe," Jacob said, "If he comes back with someone's sheep, we want to act like we do not know that animal." They all laughed at the picture.

Excitement was building for Phoebe, her first experience being away from home as a married woman. It was so wonderful that she was glowing, but Tanner just enjoyed her spontaneity. He would have let her do anything her heart wanted, for she was a woman of beauty and virtue. He appreciated her fine qualities more and more each day.

※

Upon approaching the Black Sea, the beauty of the expanse of water dazzled their eyes. They kept traveling toward Odessa. The water is so blue that it appears to be dark. "Look," shouted Jacob, "I see several ships coming into view. When arriving at the large vastness of the market area, they were somewhat surprised at the number of people. It appeared to be a whole village, but was only many families all on the same mission, buying and selling merchandise for the coming year. 'Some day,' Lesia projected, 'this will become a big city like Rome or Athens. The shipping area will bring in great wealth to the area.'" She hoped that she would live to see that day.

The men took charge, Tanner leading the way since he was the most experienced. Thinking about the last time she first met Tanner, she thought, *Yes, was it so long ago, or was it only a fortnight. No, it was a year ago.* She thought about the delicacy of her hands and lack of experience at that time, and the changes that came over the year. "Tanner, my dear, would you believe that snakes have been killed and cows milked with these hands?"

Laughing, he remarked, "Now, woman, you should learn to shoot with a bow and arrow."

"No, quibble[20] Phoebe, you are perfect just the way you are." Inwardly, she objected to them.

Suddenly, Tanner threw up his hand, hushing all talk. They were passing a dog fight, and one of the dogs looked like his old first wolf. Bohndan and Jacob gaped at the sight, while Tanner cried out, "No, no, we do not allow dogfighting in our area." Then they realized that one of the dogs was the aggressor and was attacking a farmer's hound.

"Tanner, no," Phoebe whispered. But an arrow streaked through the crowd and the ugly one lay dead.

"Thank you," the people yelled, "Next it might have been us or our children." The fur trader was only the one not happy, but he recognized old Tanner and knew that he was a talk of strength like a warrior of those parts, so he picked up the wolf and headed back away from the area.

"Keep your wolves penned, my dear friend," Tanner yelled and shot an arrow through his fur hat. "He will get the message, now." Phoebe looked at Tanner's new

---

[20] minor objection

behavior with inquisitorial[21] thoughts. She had been raised to always be kind to man or beast. Now she knew what lay in the core of her husband, not exactly sure if she liked it, but thinking too, that her hero had saved the day. Jacob was a little bit disappointed, however. He had liked being in a brawl and was hoping to finally again get to join one or perhaps watch. Phoebe, scolding twice, enjoined everyone to remember the Golden Rule.

Milling through the crowd, looking for a place to set up their wares, the weary travelers noted the many people and many makeshift boxes, used as tables to show off their wares. Oxcarts here and there were loaded with goods while blankets were hung from grapevine ropes to display beautiful works. Pots, pans, and pottery were something to behold, yet to Lesia's eyes, it didn't compare to the beauty of the markets of Jerusalem and Rome. Yet, she knew that this new country was poor and had yet to be transformed like the older cities. She wondered what all that would be like as she could see that this land held plenty of God gifts in the heart of its earth and the people that God had placed within its boundaries.

Fixing themselves something to eat, suddenly the realization fell on them that Wandering Star was

---

[21] sever questioning

missing. They concluded that it must have happen sometime in the early morning before daylight. With the people and animals moving in from Scythia in the north and the surrounding areas, noise and confusion reigned, making it hard not to be overwhelmed.

"Calm down," Lesia told herself. "Star probably just heard something and went to investigate." But her thoughts of the angry hunter with the arrow in his fur cap kept coming to her mind. "No, I will dismiss that horrid thought."

Finally, three big merchant ships could be seen setting up at different distances from each other but close enough to work the shore area. This sight generated excitement of hope for all with a year's work for bartering or selling and income coming into their area. One captain and some of his rough looking crew, toting a knife or two around each waist, rowed in to begin the bartering process. Lesia thought a good shave and haircut would do wonders for them. Those who knew the order of business stood aside to allow the animal traders to meet with the captain. First to be loaded were the horses, and then the cows, followed by the sheep and the oxen.

The crew with much care counted each animal, so Lesia was surprised when small groups of animals could swim toward the bigger ships. The crew there hauled the animals up to the ship deck and then lowered them to the bowels of the ship to await transport to other areas.

Bohdan and Tanner were told that some old rope from a main mast was being fixed. Asking about the lifting of the animals, they explained about the sheaves and axle use or type of pulley rigged for this. Then the sailor tossed them some eye—splices of rope that were going to be thrown away.

Finally, the merchandise was brought to shore. Handcrafted chairs and tables were set up for display. Pottery from Egypt and Jerusalem, clothing and many other items began the process of trading and bartering. Lesia, Phoebe, and Nadia got into the fray, cautioning each other not to take home more things than they brought. On that note, the search began for the items most needed back home.

Although many beautiful items vied for their attention, the chant of the day was focus, focus, focus.

Those who had finished their business began taking advantage of the beach area upriver from all the fuss and commotion of the business at hand. The adults were floating and swimming while the children were occupied with making sand castles. The sunny day was made for the liking of the young and the old alike. A descended evening giving one last time for a celebration. The folk dancing began and went way into the morning hours. And still there was no sign of Star.

Bohndan and Nadia decided to start looking around at several of the camps, asking if anyone had seen him. Lesia asked, "You don't think he was stolen and sold and is on that ship that just sailed away, do you?" Bohndan did not answer her but kept on walking. Jacob and Tanner went another way with heightened concern.

Then Bohndan spotted a makeshift tent constructed out of blankets in the distance near the trees. It was set apart from all the others. Placed in front of it was a stick with white strings tied around them to warn strangers that illness resided within. However, next to the tent Star was tied up to another tree.

Joining up with Bohdan and Nadia now were Tanner and Jacob. "What is going on?" Tanner question and started to walk toward the tent when Bohndan stopped him.

"Let's think this through. The illness may be catching. Even touching the straps on Star, may cause us to become ill. Star doesn't look like he's been mistreated. Bohndan paused now for some reaction from the rest of the group."

"First, let's holler to see if someone is still alive behind the blankets," Tanner suggested. A shout had its effect when crawling out the tent flap came the dirty Sam still wearing the hat with the hole in it. "You, you mangy dog. I should have put that arrow through your ugly stealing heart!"

"No, please take it away. It is a curse, and this sickness fell as soon as I tied up that animal. Please, please help me."

Looking at each other, surprised by this turn of events and astonished that there was no plague, no one moved. Then Lesia without even asking headed straight for Star and began to untie him, Jacob following to give assistance. "What do you think, Lesia? What do you suggest? A man could get hung if he stole a horse."

"No Jacob, this episode was for you and for us. This is a learning experience, and now we must share the Good News with this man who has no clue of the divine goodness of God and probably has never even considered salvation or has any knowledge of right and wrong. He has just lived his life for his own selfish desires."

Bohndan and Nadia finally came over, and Tanner still fuming, realizing that Lesia was right, told the hunter to wash his face and come back out to sit a spell. The hunter wiped some tears from his eyes as the swelling began to leave. His vision slowly returned to normal as he began to tell his story. "I was an orphan from the age of fifteen and was just living from hand to mouth. I've had to make my own way as best I could these many years." When asked about his knowledge of God, he told them that God learning was not for him. Lesia invited him to join them for supper and told him that she wanted to share the life of Andrew with him. "Andrew walked this area and died for these people whom he loved for God. You were one that Andrew would have laid down his life for, as well. He lived to explain the love of God and His plan for salvation, the giving of His Only Son, who died in Jerusalem by the hands of the Roman soldiers on a cruel cross."

Dirty Sam promised he would show up, but Tanner held back his inner thoughts, "Yeah, right. He will hightail it out of here as soon as we leave."

Star showed no worse for wear for his ordeal except he walked in a circle a couple of times, which made Nadia laugh along with some children who were watching as they passed back to their campsite. Phoebe had to hear all about the goings-on and was excited about the visitor who was coming to hear about the good news. "Don't forget to tell him about the sandals."

"Yes," said Lesia, hoping in her heart of hearts that he would show up. So many hear and then don't accept the invitation with sad results for them as their life will go on just in the same, continuing in their old habits of sin. Some people don't even realize that we are not in this present world forever.

Tanner stoked up the fire some more and reset the kettle of water for tea. He replaced a few more stones for safekeeping of the fire, meanwhile looking for the hunter. "No show," Lesia shook her head. "Maybe I should have shared everything at his campsite." She thought the scare would have been enough to make Dirty Sam start thinking about his life and spiritual living. Good nights were said, and Lesia made sure Star was tied close to her before she closed her eyes.

Phoebe looks like we better retire for the night. Tomorrow is another day and we will be returning after the last ship sails.

Jacob felt those words because he would not be going back with them.

Jacob

All the ships finally left, and here he still does not know which way he was to go. He lamented that he didn't follow through and inquire as to which way those ships would be heading. His head was not working, and now what? Go back home. He did not feel that in his soul. Early the next morning, a boat rowed up to shore. Mugface looked at what was left of a bigger crowd several weeks in the making. "Come, Samuel. Let's see if anyone is still here that needs transportation to our side of the Black Sea. If not, we shall set sail and get some fishing in for our low larder."

Meanwhile, two men nestled under their blankets were awaking and discussing how they were to travel to the north-eastern part of the Black Sea. Philip said, "The Shema and began to praise God of heaven and earth and honor Yeshua who died for him and this entire world."

"Amen," said Nathaniel as he folded up the blankets to bundle for easy carrying. "Let's go toward the shore." That's when they spotted a small vessel that had not been there the night before.

Meanwhile, the group was discussing Jacob's plight. "We promised Father that we would see that

Jacob would be secure in which way he would be going. But to just leave him here. No," said Phoebe. "You will return with us Jacob and who knows that this is the way it was supposed to be."

"No." Jacob shook his head. "This does not fit well inside my heart and soul." And on that note, he sulked away toward the sea shore.

The women had the oxcart packed and ready for the last few things that had to cool down after being on the fire. "Last call for tea anyone," Nadia called out. "Oh, Jacob is walking it off Bohndan. He'll see we are right and will be back. He is still young and lacks some patience," she commented as if she was an expert on the subject.

Star, now, where is he? "Lesia, do you have your donkey?"

"My donkey!" Lesia whipped around and with her mouth open in astonishment, "No. He was just standing beside me." As she thought about it, she realized, "Okay, he probably is following after Jacob."

"Right, so let's go also."

—◈—

"Don't look now Nathaniel, but we have a young colt donkey walking toward us. Would this be the answer to our prayer, Philip? However, as you can tell, he is still too young to have anything placed on his back."

Laughing, they continued walking and believing. "Philip, remember when Andrew had his donkey Malka with him when we last met and prayed God speed for him?"

"Yes, in fact, the color of that young one would make you think it almost matches Malka's coat."

"Yes," said Nathaniel and readjusted his bundle over his left shoulder. Star fell in step with the two men, and they just looked at each other, sensing that someone would soon come looking for it. "This reminds me of when Saul went after his father's donkeys."

"Well, I don't expect Saul," retorted Philip. "Remember those donkeys went back home."

"Yes, but didn't he meet up with some prophets who had wine and bread?" Philip gave him a look and then they both laughed.

—⁂—

Mugface talked to several people and was told of the three big ships that had come in and that so far everyone was satisfied with their purchases. "Does anyone need passage to the other side of the sea?" he inquired of several people, but the only reply was no. "Come Samuel, let's return to our boat. I must have gotten my heart message mixed up. I really thought the Lord told me to come at this hour and on this day."

When Jacob reached the shore, he stood staring at the boat that was there, wondering when it had come ashore. Turning around, Jacob greeted Mugface as he returned to his boat. Samuel and Mugface saw the young man and wondered if he was a passenger needing a ride. They greeted the young man, and Jacob introduced himself. The conversation flowed very easily, causing Mugface to know that his heart did not give him the wrong message. He knew that his young man was the object of this journey to the mouth of the river this morning.

Jacob explained he had wanted to travel to Egypt but just didn't make up his mind soon enough and now all the big ships are gone— came with family and Lesia but couldn't finish.

"Lesia, where is she? Show me. Where is she, my boy?" He did not have far to go. The troop was headed his way: Star, Philip, and Nathaniel were coming from one direction, while Lesia, Bohndan, Nadia, Tanner, and Phoebe were coming from the other direction. Now they all stood looking at one another.

Mugface, Samuel, and Lesia all started hugging each other, while the others watched in disbelief that the people Lesia had told them about were now facing them. *How has this happened?* thought Tanner. Two more men joined them by now and said good morning.

"We see that there is joy in the air and may we hope for some as we need transportation to another part of this great Black Sea."

Mugface was really excited by this time, gesturing with his hands, saying, "Of course, not all these ones are going to use my services. I knew it, I knew it, and he was for a moment into his own praise to God.

Philip and Nathaniel then introduced themselves. We are disciples of the man called Jesus, and we are carrying the good news to others as the Lord called us to do. Lesia upon hearing this blurted out, "Oh my word, did you know Andrew?" They looked at her and both replied, "Yes, he was Peter's brother and one of us as we were twelve." Wandering Star now nuzzled close to Jacob and stood behind him.

Philip putting two and two together recalled the day Andrew walked beside him with a very heavy heart. Now I wonder if she was the reason. Lesia enlightened him when she said, "I loved him till the end." Then she shared how she was in Patras where Andrew died and that she saw him taken down from that ugly cross. As her tears began to fall, Philip and

Nathaniel put their arms around her and comforted her.

"We had heard the news and were glad that a year ago we had met here and had fellowship. He mentioned that he was planning to return to Patras to encourage the new Christians and to bring in more believers in that city." Moments later, the time for departure had come so each could continue his or her own personal journey. Philip and Nathaniel asked the group if they could pray for their safe journey back to their homes and especially on the newlyweds. They again said that God has a bigger plan, and they were always surprised and filled with joy when the supernatural was at work.

Mugface and Samuel asked who was going where. Everyone turned to look toward Jacob. No one knew what to say until Philip with discernment said, "It looks like the young man is to be under our care. Son, if Jesus has called you, we will soon know for sure. Your training will come from us who have been with Jesus, whom we now know was the *word* made flesh and dwelt among us."

Then Mugface spoke up, "We shall go to my place. My homestead is on the Crimean Peninsula, and from there, we will decide on the direction God shows us. Samuel assisted them into the boat, causing him to have to walk around the sea again toward home since there was no more room in the boat. He said that would be fine as he had walked this journey many times before while growing up in this area. With that, goodbyes were said by all.

Lesia went to Wandering Star and started to lead him up from the shore to go back with her, but Star balked and went to Samuel and stood by him. "Looks like the colt is to go with me." Lesia held her breath for a moment, saddened that the colt and the sandals were now gone from her. Tears began to flow again.

Nadia and Phoebe hugged her and took the halter from her hand, holding it out to Samuel. Jacob had gotten into the boat when his heart was nudged by Lesia's act of giving him both sandals, so he stood up and bounced back over the side of the boat, splashing into the water and back up on the shore. He turned Lesia around, "One sandal, Lesia, for me and one for you and your school." He wiped her tears and reminded her that if the calling is to be, it will be. "In time, I could again be home again to help you with your school. God only knows." He hugged her again and kissed her cheek and whispered, "I'm not ready to fill his sandals yet, but with Philip and Nathaniel and Wandering Star a lot will happen, I assure you."

They watched as Mugface's boat slowly caught a nice wind. Waving together while again holding

Phoebe as her tears mingled with a last loud yell, take care of my brother. Echo back, *we* will.

Phoebe whispered, "Please, oh please, God take care of my brother." They, in silence, started their return journey toward home. Yes, home. Lesia Tkach was going home with her brother Bohndan and a dream in her heart.

Bohndan started at the head of the line, followed by Tanner and Phoebe his oxcart heavily loaded down. "Seems we are taking more back than what we brought." Phoebe laughed. Lesia and Nadia followed behind carrying some of the things that were lighter, especially some small things they had purchased for themselves.

The campfire later that night while heading home was a little subdued without Jacob and Wandering Star and of course that neighbor's sheepdog. Bohndan said, "By this time, Bo'bik could be anywhere."

The next morning, they began to talk about the plans after arriving home. Nadia mentioned that facing that Roman neighbor when they got back home was going to be a little awkward since this animal was so trained and obedient. Lesia laughed. "Well, so much for a trained dog, or even a trained donkey." And on that they both laughed. "I hope Bo'bik won't be in the family way if he does return." Lesia suddenly lost control, and her laughter made even

Bohndan stop the cart ahead and yell back, "What's so funny?"

Why does it seem that going back home is usually shorter than when you are heading out? The question was tossed around for a little bit when Lesia said, "Hurray," about the same time as Tanner's cart was turning off the main road toward the hot springs. She made no excuses this time about the water being dangerous as she was taking off shoes, then stockings, while walking down the hill toward the heated natural water. "Ah." Soon everyone had done the same. Tanner said, "We will camp here tonight and have a morning healing before we set out again." The vote was unanimous.

The road to Phoebe's father's home soon appeared. Tanner and Phoebe were excited because they would get to be man and wife in the new home he had built. "By now, Mother would have decided that this was where she could live or moved out." Tanner laughed. She just may decide to go and live with her brother, so we will be nice love, smiling at him.

Yes, Catherine was no worse for wear and remarked that the home was a delight along with the weather and Rabbi Ruben's hospitality.

The oxen too were excited, for they would be not be beasts of burden for another few days. Lesia was glad for the news about Jacob that could be shared and especially about who was taking him under their wings.

Tanner went straight toward his home along with Phoebe, so they both could decide where to place the new things. He was a little disappointed that he did not get any window help as he had heard Rome was using something, and some did not even know what he was talking about. Next year maybe was the discussion and then the scream of delight as he whisked her up into his arms and took her across the threshold and off to explore the home while she was still in his arms. Laughter and love poured over each room. Catherine had rearranged some of the rugs, and they were perfect. Everything was cleaned and dusted. Thanks, both echoed.

Rabbi waited for a little bit and then signaled that supper would start even though the young couple was absent. After a satisfying meal, Nadia and Lesia helped Dell clean up, yawing by the time they were finished. They both decided that it would be an early night for them and that they were going to enjoy inside sleeping, as well. Bohndan and Rabbi walked down toward the barn since chores never ceased.

Bohndan got the surprise of his life. Who do you suppose was enjoying a warm straw bed alongside a few sheep? Yes, that trained dog. "When did Bo'bik show up?" asked Bohndan.

"Oh, it was a couple days after you left, and it was pouring down rain. We were looking out the window, and here the dog with a mother ewe who was hurt was coming down the lane. She could go only a few steps at a time, and the dog would just sit beside her and then nip her, and she would move a few more feet. We were aghast of the sight. Wet and matted hair, we just could not understand but then sheep do wander off and fall into holes. We surmised that this happened, and the dog must have had the necessary heart to stay with the animal and to encourage it to safety along the way. The dog seemed to know or sense that this was the house to come to." Sure, sure, he was with us here!

"Well, if that doesn't beat all," he said while shaking his head. "Wait till we tell the women."

"Oh, that isn't the end. You see, she was close to birthing and for everything that is sacred and holy the little baby was born later the next day. We have named it Raindrop."

"Bo'bik was helping with the ox like he was guiding them, but in the morning, we had no dog. We called and called but to no avail.

Wonders do exist and still perplex my mind. Lesia will run with this one. You can count on that," Bohndan muttered while his head was doing more shaking, as both headed back to the house.

"No way," and out of the house ran Lesia with Nadia right behind her. The foot race was on.

"Oh, Bo'bik," Nadia said as she petted the animal. "You are one dog that I am glad to behold. She then went to look at the little lamb, Raindrop all right looking at the odd black drop on forehead. Inside her she wondered, "Oh no, it is the strange patch in the middle of its forehead." Looking at Lesia both had read each other's mind.

The dog got up like he knew that his mission was over and complete and that Bohndan had returned and now he could also return to his own owner. He followed both the women back to the house and found that the kitchen rug was just to his liking and placed his body down just to observe the humans. What they don't know I was heading home up River Road when I found the wounded sheep.

Tanner and Phoebe came over that evening and had to go down to see this miraculous sight. They looked and just shook their heads. In fact, Rabbi Ezar, finally shook his head.

Goodbyes are not easy but necessary even among loved ones. Now Lesia would be following Bohndan and Nadia, the oxcart, and Bo'bik. She knows now when she gets back it will be mentally slow for her after what has transpired. She now will be a family member in a brother's home, not just a guest in a farmer's home. Here with loved ones she now can start thinking about her own place—her future.

The welcome home was unbelievable as it seemed that all the animals, including the chickens, mooed, brayed, and clucked their greetings. When Bo'bik was returned, the neighbor was amazed when told the story about his faithful dog and the mother sheep. Speculus said, "He is a mighty serious dog when he takes the flock into his care and watch. He must have heard the sheep's cry, but I really can't tell you how he did it. I never knew a dog would stay with one sheep like that. From now on, we shall make sure this one is treated with extra care, right Dylan.

Nadia was also glad to be back to familiar surroundings. *Camping out*, she thought, *makes me appreciate the comforts of home.* The best of that was bringing back helping aids for this farm life.

And one is some help on how to dry the clothes outside instead on small spikes pounded in the side of the shed.

Late that night, Lesia sat up, went to her back pack, and slipped out the Andrew's left sandal. She wondered what Jacob would be learning and how the right sandal would be used. Miracles have happened when God leads his chosen ones. She just could not get to sleep as her mind began to dwell on events past and present. She finally got up and headed toward the kitchen. Maybe some warm milk would help her. She pretended that Andrew was across the table from her, and she talked about Wandering Star. Out loud she speaks, "What part will Jacob or Andrew's friends contribute? Did Andrew tell them about me? They seemed to know a little bit."

"Andrew, my body feels very tired and old right now, and you would know all about that since you did so much, walking the rough terrain to find the people dispersed over the land. I still love you, fisherman," and on that she returned to her room and to sleep.

Somewhere during the night, she began dreaming of when she was a little child and began some studies with Herodias' daughter with a pleasant and firm lady. Lady would then bow as a kind greeting to Mara Chin and remarked, she did very well today.

She remembered the interest and the excitement of learning along with social learning, but Salome was more interested in her beauty and dancing. What was her name? Can't remember her name. Can't remember?

Her dream took another twist, and she could now see children of many ages, sizes and colors all together. She began to toss and turn as some of the children were crying and reaching toward her with dirty hands and trying to get her to hold them. Finally, she woke up, her forehead broken out in a sweat. The dream disturbed her, but she finally shook the images, throwing back one of the blankets to cool down the bedding, and tried returning to sleep.

Yawning in the morning, Lesia stumbled into the kitchen area. Nadia was ready to ask her how she slept but stopped because she could see that Lesia did not have a good night. "Want to talk?"

After the second cup of tea made from one of the teas bought from merchant ship, Lesia began to talk about the dream and wondered why she would have a nightmare about schooling when schooling for her had been the breath of spring air. She wished she could have gone on and on, learning more and more. In fact, she aspired of becoming a top-rated teacher of young ones even though boys are favored in learning.

Nadia just sipped her tea and nodded wanting Lesia to go on. Okay, Lesia, maybe your dream is a message for you, directing your life now since marriage doesn't seem to be an option for you? You have been teaching and working with children one on one recently.

"It would be a soul filling job, but the children in my dream were crying and of different peoples, so I'm confused. It's too much for me to handle right now, so I'm going out to work in the barn to feed Ahava and talk to her. Don't set my plate for breakfast. I couldn't eat if I had to."

"Good morning, my lovely one," Lesia said, smiling. "You look like you are waiting to hear about what happened to your baby boy. Well, he is going with two friends of Andrew's and with Jacob. Does the Creator plan things that are beyond human understanding?" Yes, he does, hugging her head again.

Ahava neighed like saying, "You got that right." Lesia hugged Ahava and started brushing her coat. She thought back to the time when Ahava pulled Alma Delores's ribbon from her hair, and the children played and chased her. She thought about the multifarious reasons for the children becoming orphans and the problems that each one encountered. Was this part of the message in the dream? She finished up her work in the barn by spreading hay and removing the manure. Then she gathered the eggs.

"Whew, lady, you must have something on your mind big time because you charged into these chores without even stopping to leave something for me to do," Bohdan quipped smiling.

"Oh, yes, I do. I guess Nadia told you about the dream or rather the nightmare I had last night. What do you think?"

"Don't know, Lesia. I've heard it said that if you have a dream reoccur a couple of times, it really was a message for you. Wait and see if it happens again. Right now, I am going to open the back gate and let the animals run the range a little bit. Hurry, and you can still have that biscuit that I left on the plate and count yourself lucky." As he went toward the back of barn, he saw that Ahava had it already opened. "That donkey," he muttered under his breath.

Washing up, Lesia felt better and the work had really helped make her hungry and not only the biscuit but she ate two more along with two eggs and bacon. "Whew, at that rate I will be like a good old fat farmer's sister."

Nadia laughing said, "Well, let's go do the laundry now and lose some of it."

"Okay, give me just a moment as some of my clothes need to be done." The wind was great with its whipping the homemade shirts, blouses, and underclothes—the towels acted like dancers.

Bohdan had rigged up from the ship's old frayed rope from their mast, together using the short loose ones to get a good long one and God blessed the tree limbs that held the ends.

"Yuk…folding and folding," Lesia expressed. "No, Nadia, smoothing out clothes not my best job, but if I did not smooth or press out some of the wrinkles on her tunic, I usually hid it but was finally smacked on the wrist and had to go without supper for that day. Old Hateful."

Laughing, Nadia promise she would not beat her but realized some of the abuse she had endured even in a rich woman's employment.

The smell of sun dried linen cloths and sewn cases of cloths for holding the down of ducks and other for straw refreshed along with nicer mats and lovely stiched items. *Yes, freshly made bed makes for a good sleep tonight*, she thought as she blew out her candle and fluffed her new manmade cloth filled with soft sheep wool for her head.

Would she dream the same dream, and if she did, what would it mean? She hugged the sandal and placed it beside her and was soon asleep.

The next day rain kept them in the house after chores, but since it was great for the crops and the flowers, they were content. Then Bohndan discusses Catherine, a sister that was injured from an ox that was stung on the nose and jerk back into the cart and Catherine was tossed to the ground hitting her head. She has a better memory now, Tanner told him, but for a while I thought we were going to lose her completely. Tanner is going to bring her for a visit to stay for a while, but he says he just goes slowly with her in doing things.

He was very pleased that she finally agreed to live with him and Phoebe. She said that when she saw you, Lesia she thought for a minute it was mother and dropped her tin plate.

So, it is my mother that I look like. Oh, what a delight to hear. She kept staring at me, but I let on that I wasn't noticing—so that was the reason—oh my goodness she may not remember me as a young baby but nevertheless we now have her and she will soon be staying awhile with us and on that everyone agreed with a big yes and who knows being around me and you she may remember more and more and that will be just wonderful. Lesia finally stopped and caught her breath.

"Now where is that apple pie that you two spent time on baking this morning? Oh, food always a man's thing." Nadia laughed. "Put some sweet cow's milk over it if you want to. I enjoyed mine that way."

"Next was a good time for mending and stitching on her ideas about how she wanted some of her clothing to help doing the chores a little bit easier. Yes, time for chores and then bedtime, I am really getting into this farmer way of living," she said, laughing to herself.

After a rain, the air smelled fresh and the grass seemed to grow overnight, so they surmised that by tomorrow or the next day Bohndan would let the animals graze in the front yard.

Weeds though were gotten out by hand pulling and bending of the back or your knees—better after a rain had softened the soil. She had learned to remember to do the flower garden and garden plants now after a good soaking kind of rain.

So tomorrow she mentioned that she would go first to the flower garden and maybe do some pulling of little stalks that were called suckers around the corn. The soil can be loosed by using that new funny kind of stick attached to a metal iron arrow shape, she jokes and said, "I was afraid of it and didn't want to kill the corn stalks but it did get a wasp."

Early the next day when Lesia was feeding Ahava and brushing her down, the neighbor boy, came into the barn and asked if he can have some eggs for his father. "Why yes, anytime and would you like to help me collect them?"

"Yes," he exclaimed excitingly.

"Oh, by the way what is your name?"

"Don, uh, Tus but on ship they called me Lost Goose because they said I made a lot of noise because I was crying, but Papa Spec calls me Dylan now."

"Well, Dylan, let's go over to that table and grab that round basket. Just give me just a minute here to finish up and hang up my brushes," she said, feeling some real empathy already for this child.

"Can I help put them away?"

"Certainly. Put that big one on the biggest nail. Good. Now how many brushes did we hang back up all nice and neat?" She realized that she had put out her question from her working with children.

Uggh, he just shrugged up his shoulders, pointed, and said, "That one and that one and that one."

Oh, my, she thought, finally realizing he could not count. Then she wondered if he even knew his words and how his speech is hard to understand. She motioned him to follow, and they headed toward the rustic shed for the chickens. Dylan began cooing over the babies and asked if he could pick up one. "You surely can, but hold it gently. Yes, you're doing a good job."

Asking him to count the chicks was tempting but would be cruel, so they went over to start the egg hunting. "We just let them lay, and they pretty much have set up a pattern for us, so look over in the right corner you see that the hay is made into a round shape with a little less in the middle, okay?" And then he saw the eggs and with that he gently placed the eggs into the basket she was holding and Lesia was enjoying the togetherness with again a beautiful child. "To start anything you start with the count of one," so with that thought she picked up one egg. Dylan saw this egg. He shook his head yes. "Then say with me one, one and now put up one of your fingers—no, just one." And soon he could do it up to three. "Well, my young man, we better get these eggs to your mother so I will go with you, how's that?"

"Oh, I have no mother. She died when I was little." This news shook Lesia to the core. Mother or not, a child needs to learn in this day and age, and she was the one to let his father see that point."

This frontier was a far cry from the newer cities, yet sad times are found everywhere. Dylan and Lesia chatter on the way to his home. He picked up a stone to throw and Lesia again ask how many and his lesson was on again. Finally, they were walking up the long path heading toward the front door-the farm looks not too bad for no woman around as she was surprised that the clothes were hung very neat and blowing in the wind. Yes, she could see chilton and loincloth and looked like a very nice cloak, on a roman wicker frame. I have not seen those since I left Rome.

Arriving at the door, Lesia knocked and was surprised by a shirtless man. He was by his shape a gladiator. She had seen a few at the arena shows that Herodias ordered her to attend to wait on her whims, but here? He was awkward as she and then he left and returned with his short sleevless chilton. "Wash day, my lady," he smugly said, enjoying her face as she surveys his muscles.

Then in recognition, she said, "So, sir, you look like a Roman gladiator, but kind sir, what are you doing here in this area?" Then taking another good look at her, older now like him but still beautiful. "I should ask, what are you doing here?"

"You go first."

Our Roman empire expanding to these parts especially the southern near and around the Black Sea since the fire that was a good time to leave that lower area and come north. Rome has no use for wounded animals or humans so they kept me in employment by sending me as far away as they could. My job was to spy on the people. Nero, mentioned especially if they were Christians, had high hopes my boy for you he kept saying. Ya right, it was the money he could earn on me.

"Papa Spec, lady brought me home," and he began to talk about the baby peeps, "and then she walked me home with the eggs they are in that basket she is carrying, and Papa, she showed me how to—" He turned toward the child, and with a cross look and with a shove, he gruffly muttered, "Stop, child and go feed Bo'bik."

That was too much for Lesia. She felt herself getting angry and now her arm raised and her finger pointed. How dare you…you overgrown beast shoving your child and speaking so mean. You also are so selfish that it is all about you and your problem, but you neglect your own child's schooling-shame, shame since you are a Roman."

He grabbed her hand and on that she backed away and turned to leave. If he would not listen about

Dylan, she would do something even if he objected. She was so angry.

He then remembered a young lady who sat with Queen Herodias at one such match. "You, stop, you were there," he blurted out. She turned back as she was heading for home.

"I was where?" she strongly asked, still ready to punch his lights out. "Whoa here, truce," went her thoughts. "What happened to the commandment to show love to thy neighbor? Ouch."

She came back up the path as now he was walking toward her, and she now could see he had a limp with his foot. Now he was face to face with her.

"Rome, the day a match with gladiator against gladiator. We were the show for that day. We had to draw lots, and it was to the death. My friend drew my lot. Our hearts were saddened, but we knew the training ritual at the Ludus Gladiator Training School. Our school master made sure we heard all about Spartacus and Flamma and many others before us. We knew that the crowd could yell, 'Lugula' (kill him) at any time it felt the desire for blood. We ate barley and chose our own weapons, yet we were like fine race horses for Rome, especially for Nero. Emperor Titus had his favorite pair Prescus and Venus. Most of them were not citizens but were slaves from other areas. I chose this field to please my own desires. Yes, wine, women, and fame. We were to win for Rome, the goddess Minerva, and of course Nero. Yes, I was Speculus the Great.

"I remember a young lady sitting beside a heavy woman that was a queen and heard that the queen was to let that young lady be a sport prize for a selected gladiator. She and Nero had chosen me, but somehow, and to my chagrin, my foot slipped and my friend had the knife to my neck. Then I could hear the crowd and knew it was thumbs down. He read my eyes and paused, pulled me up by the hair, and plunge the knife into my left foot penning my foot to the dirt in the coliseum. Wounding me was a disgrace to me, also causing him to fight another battle. The crowd was ugly and fickle and blood thirsty, wanting to see a death. I heard the booing as I limped toward the inner gate. You were there. Tell me that wasn't you!"

Nervous now she gets a quick mental thought of that terrible day, oh yes, but was commanded there in body, but mentally my thoughts were elsewhere— really did not care for that kind of sport and was about to explain more– (glad *Herodias chose her willing daughter Salome)* but he then smiled, *"so it looked like the gods have you yet to be considered in my life."* Flirting *with her.*

"Please forgive me for my unruly tongue," Lesia quickly remarked, "but your son…"

"No, my dear lady, he is not mine. He was abandoned and was on the ship that left to sail from Rome to Fair Haven. He was to become a cabin boy, but I said no. He is a Roman child."

Now her feelings about the young boy were full-blown in her soul. The problem was worse than she had first thought when realizing his lack of learning but worse than that now his lack of a mother's love and country.

The silence spoke volumes for a few seconds then he also knew the softer side of himself. He proceeded to thank her for bringing Dylan home. "I am going to when I go back to Rome to see what I might find out about orphans, and thank your husband for the eggs."

"No, no. Bohndan is my brother, but please, I love children and am teaching along with chores, smiling, and if you will let Dylan, come over for an hour or two, I would like to begin lessons with him. Already just today he has learned to begin counting." Her eyes spoke of her love of teaching, so he agreed with her request, and then limped toward the barn. She sensed that he felt half the man he used to be in Rome and felt compassion for him.

Speculus, called himself after a famous gladiator, became a regular visitor along with Dylan. Speculus shared about why he now call the boy Dylan. "Well, why didn't you just ask the child? Well, it sounds funny, but one old sailor said the child sounds like a *lost goose*. He with his crying and being afraid probably in pronouncing his name got out don-hiccup-t-hiccup-us so with all the bawling *Lost Goose* was what they tag him on board. Well, fine lady there were some other names, I won't mention. We all laugh on the ship calling him that for a while. Then someone mention an old deceased Greek friend that died the same time the boy was found. In memory of him, we gave Lost Goose the name Dylan, meaning sea, and fine lady that Greek name is just for now."

"Poor child named Dylan. A Roman child, now with a Greek name, really, his mother, he did not tell you about his mother? Look at me, you did not ask, did you?"

Then in defense he said, "He was an orphan, so no, I did not." Men, then she paused. "No, I am glad you took him, but we must change that image he has about himself, because he is showing good smarts along with a gift to draw. Really!"

"I did some paperwork for boarding and did use D. Donu Tus.

What we thought sounded like 'don-u-Tus.'"

Donatus, means given, was used then for his boarding pass to travel that was accepted.

Speculus, with a still small voice inside, said, "What if this boy is not Roman? I just assume that on board."

A year went by, and Speculus had begun to understand from Lesia and the Bohdan's about their Christian walk and about Lesia and the events of her life. He knew he was smitten from the moment she pointed her finger at him and felt unworthy as a man. He never expected this to happen on just another riding outing with her.

However, it did happen when they, after a fast race, rested his animals on top of a lovely country hillside. Lesia's loveliness along with her fragrance was too much for him to control the desire in his heart. He quickly moved his horse beside hers and reached over, pulling her from her horse and into his arms. He kissed her mouth, taking her protest away, finally feeling her body give the signal of consent. He caressed her neck with his lips, her eyebrows, and then her ear at which point she moaned, "Andrew."

Andrew? This jerked him back into reality. He sat her upright and then placed her back on her own horse. "Andrew, Andrew? No, I am not Andrew. Lesia, the man is dead for heaven's sake. Your God I can serve, but a dead man? Who can fight that? No way, my lady, no way." He kicked his horse into a quick gallop, his heart feeling the pain of a gladiator's knife cutting his throat.

She sat a moment contemplating on what had just happened. She was going to give him the left sandal to wear on his impaired foot so that it would be restored, but what he loudly said was right. She now also wanted more. She slowly wiped her eyes and said, "Andrew, what we had will never leave a part of my heart, and I am afraid I have lost again."

She purposed in her heart that if Jacob returned with the Andrew's other sandal that would be a sign. She vividly remembered the old lady's request for her to promise to give the sandals to someone who had a need. She also knew that Jacob was in line for them to wear. "Yes, I promise!" Lesia reaffirmed. But whom? Would that change? But when?

She felt still the passion as she rode back toward her brother's farm and wondered what God would do about it. Wiping more of her tears away from her face, she was hoping that no one saw them. No people but in the distance pasture Ahava and Bo'bik with the angel, they knew.

She slipped off Speculus horse he had given her to ride and was remembering the day he gave it to her. He had purchased it from the Roman stables at a high price. The horse ran like the wind, and she called him Mighty Wind during the race usually winning and feeling young again; that time was special. She loves laughter and Speculus has a hearty and loud one, which she enjoyed every time.

Andrew, am I slipping away from God? Isn't finding happiness in this life important? But again, one that does not want to go all the way with you God is also in your word, darkness cannot fellowship with light. Right now, I feel excited and mixed up, very, very, embarrassed.

"Go home, pretty one," she whispered as she patted Mighty Wind (Pegasus*) again and readjusted the reins not to drag, go on home. "This may be the last day I will ride you," and Pegasus felt small wet drops hit the side of his face.

She starts a prayer to God who is love that His will in her life would be completed, according to His perfect plan for her. She slipped into the house and went directly toward her room. She wondered where she might find out how women dealt with heart issues like this. Looking now at Andrew's sandal and knowing that a holy connection has been working for her, destination of her life started here as a baby infant, life intervened for her safety not for selfish reason but that she might have some chance at education consisting now of more men than women, and now she can help the children of this country where her roots were from the beginning.

Andrew and I never knew the root connections but God-sky does and now I am love smitten again but will deal with this tomorrow. Picking up the sandal and placing it down at her feet for right this moment out of respect, she can't hug it.

Her dream was back in Jerusalem where John Mark mentions about the women being perplexed when going to Jesus tomb and finding it empty. They were in love with Jesus and then two angels ask them why to do you seek the dead among the living? He is risen (Luke 24:4).

She remembers hearing how strong then those women were, especially Jesus's mother. Why tonight of all times to remember. It must be the sandal. *Okay, Andrew. I will remember you are alive but not here on earth.* Soon sleep came while tears slowly slid down her face.

"Bohndan it has been a month, and she is not herself. I'm worried."

"Nadia, you are not going to believe this, but Spec had placed a note at the barn, but I didn't see it and today I almost tossed it out with the soiled straw. Here, read this. He is giving the horse to her. Do you think in her mental state we want her riding? Well, going to show her this note in the morning. Is she in love again?"

"Bohndan, what do you think? Time will tell, Nadia, time will tell."

Little did they know that Lesia had overheard this and whispered a part of something is better in love than zero. What do I have? One sandal and one horse. She went back to bed.

Riding Mighty Wind did help but passing by the farm brought a sadness. One day she just let out her feeling openly in her room while packing and unpacking some things, disturbed again by her dream. She had also confirmed to start looking for a place for her orphanage.

"Mr. hard heart loser can be damned for hell. For all I care, he will probably let Dylan grow up and live in the Roman's slums among the uneducated while he enjoys his free love attitude. He doesn't care, why should I? Who needs the likes of, look at my muscles either, why do I care and why am I praying for this heathen? Dylan, God, remember sweet Dylan. Don't let the hurt of a grown man affect that bright lad. God please forgive my hate and anger right now." Turning, she saw Nadia watching her little show.

"Perhaps you are falling in love with Mr. Hard Heart. Show me, muscles heathen, can't believe you called him that." Grinning, she said, "Time for lunch."

Nadia has been watching for some time the friendship of those two growing and the abrupt leaving of Speculus made her question why but thought that was for the child, but then Lesia's mood changes and now this little behavior scene she straight out asked Bohndan.

"Do you think Lesia is falling in love?"

"Time will tell," he said as he hung up his hat. "Time will tell!"

Speculus Sudano (The Mighty One of Rome's Gladiators)

Listed as a fighter against Flamma the Syrian gladiator and Crixus a gallic gladiator

Burning Memory

Riding back to the barn from the embarrassing ride on the hill, his whole body was in distress. Sleep tonight-he knew would be useless. He without thinking reached for the shovel to start doing the cleanup work that was for the next day. My life is like this mess I am throwing in a heap to burn, his thoughts flung at his brain, as his enraged body, threw more soiled loads out the back door.

He kept verbally talking out loud, "how do you fight with a man who is GOD in her eyes? Calm came slowly as he suddenly just out of habit, stroked the side of Lucky' face while giving her oats. Feeling his authority now as a man was returning he amble toward the house with a heavy spirit.

Lesia doesn't know what restraint it is for me to stand my ground with having her in sight and seeing her beauty. I hear in my head her melodious laughter when we rode together and when she brings Dylan back to the house.

I use my chair for something to hold on to for strength, so that I will not kiss her again. My desire to embrace those lovely lips is strong until I remember her calling out Andrew's name. Now I am wondering would she want a man whose right foot is crippled and ugly looking. A failure as a man, what the gods call disgrace.

Donatus seems now under her spell showing possible a love child connection to her enough to mention several times, wish she could be my mother. Must end this for the child as well, for we both cannot have her.

As early morning was breaking into another lovely day, he walked out onto his raised makeshift porch he had built; taking a sip of his tea knew the final decision.

This is what he was going to do, Donatus[22] must be taken back to Rome to seek information true or not about his name. His name he was trying to say to the crew on ship was jumbled because of his crying which did not help his speech problems.

When he saw me, he ran to me, I must have looked far more trusting than the others he was facing in his

---

[22] earlier name crying with problem on ship

orphan state. Then leaving this child I just couldn't so brought him home. To make things easier for me, I kept thinking about a name. Son of the sea in Welsh is Dylan, and it was on the sea that I first set my eyes on a bawling child. Yes, will call him Dylan, rather than what the crew suggested shaking his head as his mind replayed that day in his mind.

Now unknowing is what Fate does behind the scenes in lives unaware of the strong supernatural weaving of lives. Love the biggest weaver of all.

Leaving for the sake of the child, on that reason and for that reason, will save face Speculus said verbally. Saving face-laughing, he then remembers hearing this one from what his Chinese friend would say in an embarrassing situation. Bow and grin and say, must leave-ancestor needs me, exit quickly.

Rome is where I should be and would be if it wasn't for the unfortunate day in the coliseum. It seems now a fading memory except when he looks at his foot. Thankful for some of the glory parts a-special gold gift-that he gave to his lovely mother now wrapped away in the back of the barn in an old trunk.

He a trained professional knew you do the hardest and unpleasant jobs first, so his mental list began, stop the lessons.

How do I say this, "No, more lessons to this child? His shoulders shrug as he sighs, I must and now two, pack. He then went to look for his shipping trunks. Yes, doing this, will be easier on us both.

Zeus understands my inner thoughts *the thought of never no never to look upon Lesia anymore* brought now a lump into his throat, this is hard for a grown man let alone for a motherless deprived child. Meanwhile he mentally encourages himself for sailing back to Rome, letting his mind remember all the glory with his friends in Rome and yes, don't forget Spain. Yes, his friends will be willing like before to take his calling card anytime of the day. Yes, he felt he was the man of the hour now and surely, they would have missed the charming gladiator.

A brain overload, spent from exhaustion and mentally tired from the problem, he tries as calmly as he could to explained to Dylan after supper.

It is time to go find information or papers on who you are. What would happen if we found a brother or sister. Wouldn't that be great. Dylan on that note, was shaking his head in an unsure way. Little did he know it might be the last time in this lovely quaint farm house in the Ukraine.

Dylan had a mind of his own, watching for a chance when Papa Spec was at nap time. He sneaked over to see Lesia. He told what Spec was going to do. She reassured him that this was a good thing for him and encourages him to help Spec do this and finally pulled the child to her. She wiped tears from his face-gave him mother hugs and comfort. He left with a better little heart because of her kindness and her kisses and hugs and the written work to study on his voyage, which he hid for a while, and never would anyone replace Lesia.

Third on list, the farm and my beautiful horse and the dog were uppermost as Spec headed toward the nice and large farmstead of the Tkach. He will speak to Bohdan about their care and give him some payment for anything else that Bohdan might and should do. Hoping he wouldn't encounter Lesia before this was all settled.

He asked Bohdan if he could leave Bo'bik and Pegasus in his care for taking them would be a lot of trouble. He really wanted Dylan to be the main course of action and went on about Dylan. "Sure will," said Bohndan. He was more than happy to encourage him and remarked about how much Lesia and Nadia kept saying he should see about that boy. "So, don't worry about anything you can count on me" and gave him his hearty handshake, as a promise.

Knowing down deep this will help Spec to feel you made the right decision but inside his own mind, was saying finally this man was stepping up to his duty. How happy Nadia will be but Lesia don't think so. Spec said it was Dylan but was wondering as he has seen the cold war going on.

Ahava, hearing Spec and Bohndan, knew the reason why the return to Rome.

The Hill.

———

No women had spurned him. Rome has some of the most beautiful among women, but not like her. Why, why, does THIS one get to him and her God also? No, he swore as he kicked the chair and hit his fist together. He reminded himself who he was, distant relation to Julius Caesar's cousin and was honored among the strong. His future was the glory of Rome's coliseums and gold. He knew then what he wanted to do from his mental pep talk again, and began in earnest, packing the trunks for Rome.

Leaving early, trunks and Dylan rode on Lucky, the black older horse toward the River Road and as fate would have it a ship was sailing into the Black Sea. Seeing the ship now and leaving for Rome was for real. Again, the mind did its dance in his head. Just in time for a mixed up emotional-mind searching-struggle-he faces with a love crisis in his life", no I am not leaving, yes – I AM leaving – I am the great-Gladiator with a gold belt to prove the point. His mind chose this achievement to win the argument again – two passages to Rome one-way captain sir.

Dylan was a little bit hesitant and started to cry, oh no, Dylan no one is going to laugh this time. Not with papa Spec on board, right and a fatherly touch came from his soul as he picks up Dylan and placed him on his back as he tackles the job of comforting a growing child plus handling, Dylan's personal luggage and walks like he has done this all his life-onto the ship and toward their cabin.

The journey was better than Spec expected as Dylan who is a year older and with his schooling from Lesia Dylan turned out to be quite the star on this voyage. Spec wonder if this might be what Lesia would call a God-sky event.

Spec was also trying to put the picture together without asking Dylan how he came to have those lessons. Dylan had to talk to her but when and what time is the question? Later Dylan may tell me about it.

Rome

Spec went right to his villa and after showing Dylan around the place and then the city. Leaving the next day to have some time with Council and then investigate the orphan school. Meeting Mrs. Vita Severo he liked her immediately for her smile was warming and her manners spelled confidence.

She said she would do her best pondering on the small information *on one piece of paper* – a name: Donatus and the ship where he was first discovered.

Dylan would get some schooling while he was here in Rome, she encourages Spec with his time he could decide to revisit family and friends.

The day arrived for Spec to take Dylan to the school, he was a little shy and did not say much. When Spec started to leave Dylan was hesitant of being left but Vita with her smile took Dylan's hand and suggested going to get their special dinner with a treat at the end, he went right along.

Huh, if Vita knew my family-not so good-but friends-good idea – My distance relatives and crazy Nero, maybe he will be going that way himself between good and evil. So far <u>crazy</u> had a jump ahead.

He was glad that Bohndan was going to check on Pegasus and the note I left for him to find and if he does will he give to Lesia. *I want this horse to belong to Lesia Tkach, if she wants her*-Speculus the Great.

Remember again, her hair flowing loose and flying around her head in the wind of the moment when a good stiff breeze came out of nowhere. She was at times a sore loser if she did not beat me. Women-although-he was sort of smiling on the thought – because he could have ridden his own horse, Pegasus.

He received a letter one day to come to the school, so he quickly went to find out what the news might be:

Severs School, Vita mistress on her door. Vita seeing him quickly motion for him to come in and have a seat.

The school was helpful in discovering information. He was very excited to hear Vita saying "this child only found living relative was Welsh and Italian, Mr. Dillon Daedalus) had left the English Isles working on ships. His daughter Teresa Daedalus fell ill, and the orphanage gave merit to the child and its papers, as boy child, Daedalus – no marriage-no father listed. Teresa Daedalus father listed as Dillion Daedalus merchant sailor. No first name listed so looks like the last name is what the child tried to say Donatus. We looked up that name Spanish or Italian. Teresa might have call him her little Donato or Donatello, meaning gift from God. She could have told him you are my Donato *my gift* and that could be what he thought was his name. We feel that if that was to be his given name she would have listed it. She also maybe wanted to do it later when her own heartache was calmer. She may have wanted to give the father's name to the child, anyway destiny only has shown us so little of his life.

Mr. Dillon Daedalus could take him apparently and they had watched him for a little while until Mr. Daedalus was back in the area.

Little did the orphanage know that the old man, had picked up too much illness in his life and his heart from grog and night life finally ended. Leaving then a child who when nervous cannot express himself.

The day you found him is the day and date he boarded that same ship you were on with his grandfather. The rest of the story you have," I believe that Dillon apparently fell ill and possibly had heart problems. The child afraid oh my-he certainly would be bawling-think about it. I am so glad you were the chosen one that was aboard the ship that fateful day.

We also have accepted the name you gave – Dylan-a very good welsh name we found out, so fitting-you were-we believe the angel that was chosen to help this child, smiling at him with admiration. Strange how things we don't understand happen-handing Spec the legal papers on Dylan to attend permanently, her school.

You may adopt the child if you so desire as taking him away from you now would be cruel. Apparently, Teresa was not married. So, you have the rights to this child and we are so happy, for he is quite a bright lad and loves you.

They reassured him to go on with his daily affairs and take your time in making your decision. She and the other teachers will help Dylan to settle any other problems. So far, he seems to be settling in quite nicely-smiling "just watch and see he'll thrive in our atmosphere of learning. Thanking Speculus again for his generous offer for Dylan's keep and continued schooling.

Now with Dylan accepted full time in school, he was really, free and free he would be! He headed toward the Big hot bathing Spa of the times, right in the middle of Rome.

Now his one long coliseum friend Martha with her close friend Rita, knew how to entertain the inside crowd, the fun and game society and were in full fun and play as he joined them.

Rita though was always waiting on a Spanish ship Captain-Spec kept telling her they have a friend in every port. Martha has a shape like a Queen-but she did not mind my limp and I did not mind her girth.

He really wasn't ready to party-yet-he found himself in Spain. His friends from the Gladiator school who settled to Spain's glamour did welcome him. He finally tried to renew the gladiator image and glory and when that got boring he went back to Rome and Martha. Here he added wine, and more hot spas and friends to that mental picture like the old days-glory renewed warrior I am better than ever-that was going to happen!!-wrong again failure.

Finally, the fun was no fun and he settled in on looking for livable items and usable wares for his little homestead in Ukraine. He also thought if Dylan comes back with him a better sleeping arrangement for the child would be first on the list. A job that was going to be done. Dylan is a great kid and love was growing in his heart for this child.

The God of Lesia, he has come to realize was not going away and made him afraid inside himself, yet, could it be possible that his life would be savable? Was this a big part of realizing fun like the old days was not fun at all but glorified lust. Would this God make a new man out of him a trained killer if he needed to be-hit your chest, for Rome, for Zeus! Kill-thumbs down!

He had some skills especially in seeing how things could be fixed or rearranged for the better, and when a break down came in the water systems one day in the spa he was the one they yell for-hey, can you fix this mighty one.

Visions of helping Lesia kept coming nightly-his gifts mentally-seeing how she could do things in her school, how from group training the way to add extra space when space was needed and extra strength to hold a new structure and heaven knows his work with the spa's water system, and her lifting heavy stones, don't think so, I have lifted over 300 lbs. Her being away from her brother and a lone, single, woman too all mingling inside the mind, in the late hours of the night.

Finally, he got out of bed and took a walk to quickly push all this from his mind. When more started he then decided to open the wine bottle to push away the night-then for some strange reason-decided to put it away. Lesia's was the thoughts again and unknowing to him her God, that brought sleep.

Then, as morning came he had a list of items and supplies and inside an excitement about how to use those supplies. A new kind of attitude and confidence was rising in his soul, what I do – I do right he mumbles to himself and to the mershants who put this question to him.

Can you pay for this?

His thoughts are, you bet on it plus-the money to get it all <u>and</u> <u>all the other</u> supplies you will ship me later.

Leaving several merchants, that attitude in him even tries to whistle, he finally laughs to himself but rememebers the sailor Samuel who could do it from the crow's nest inside or outside hanging while the ship was rocking on high seas.

Remembering again what happened to shake some sense into him, his mind went again to his double dare friend who with drink was somewhat careless but never the less he went riding with his tough friends to the small arena.

The friend suggested let's play I am the beast and you are the gladiator who will win, do or die, fencing with Sabers was the name of the game. He wanted to ride on horses, but I said no.

One blow was close and Speculus though with his limp was glad that this was not for Nero, for death would have been for certain. So, having enough he informed everyone by throwing his saber with his warrior cry-my visit has ended and hitting his chest twice, I bid farewell my friends and myself-Zeus speed home to Rome.

Finally, after months away, arriving back at his villa, a letter arrived.

Guardian Speculus Sir,

We really regret to inform you that Dylan ran off and we had to search for him. He was more frightened than hurt. He did have an outside experience seeing the poor side of Rome.

He apparently did something that he feels would be a punishing action that would require the parent to accept the discipline or the end of his schooling. We feel this was a direct play to have us contact you. He several weeks ago, starting to shy away from eating all his food. We just thought he was missing you and would adjust again and be his happy self.

He seems very upset that he scared us, but we assured him that you would come, and everything would settle and of course we don't want to expel him. We have grown quite fond of him. We also inform him that your whereabouts were unknown and as soon as our letter is read you will come.

So sorry to send this letter out to your villa now-as we wish to have sent it sooner. Inquiring about-no one was sure of your whereabout until docking of the Spanish ship this morning.

Come quickly if possible.

Sister Vita Severo

Back At The School

Hearing from the school of his running away Spec went quickly to inquire of the matter. Spec was surprise yet relieved to see him looking taller and showing promise of good looks. The school report spoke well of him and his grades, but his unhappiness is sorely apparent said Vita. He told me one day he misses the young lady who always let him count chicken eggs. He really talks as if she was his mother, who I know from his records died from an illness. Dillon who was watching him, as we know died on the ship when you found the boy hiding.

We could make arrangement for him to return with you-you're the only father image he will know-You have already struggled with him earlier in his life for over a year which I feel from this automatically came his love for you-but if you have decided not to take him, he will have to be told.

We know that adjustments sometimes take longer with children permanently left here. We shall hope for the best adjustment yes-if you decide to leave him.

Not wanting to overstep her hearts wish-of please Spec-see this child wants to leave and go home and be your son-she swallows her words.

Vita added quickly more about what Dylan missed. He talks about his dog Bo'bik wanting to run and play fetch-along with maybe getting some sheep-the funny donkey Ahava, that makes him laugh.

Yes, he fell in love with your place and the young lady who was beginning to teach him his letters.

Spec told her he would give her an answer by noon tomorrow. Her speech became visions of time back in Ukraine and gripped his inner self.

His quarrel is not taking this child but going back to face Lesia. A woman whose braided hair was now loose blowing in the wind etched like fire in his brain. His meeting on the hill top with Lesia, his kiss, her refusal of him for a dead man and for a God who loves everyone was becoming his nightmare.

He left and headed to check on the ships that posted their destinations and time of departures. Maybe a God-sky event will happen, and the ship will be heading right for the big Spring Sale of Ukraine.

Dylan's information on how unhappy he is and being unhappy himself was just the push that gave him the reason to head back to Ukraine, but underneath it was HER!

He now admitted to himself, he was missing his own quiet farm and down deep missing her. He headed back to the school and with some signing of paperwork picked up a child that started grinning from ear to ear. He kept saying just wait Vita I am going home and when I am older I will come back and see you right papa Spec. Yes, I answer of course son you now have your Roman rights. Vita watched as they walked out and headed down toward the docks. Pulling out her hanky she wiped a few tears away that fell freely-again feeling her job blessings and its heartaches.

Reflection From Lesia

At Bohndan and Nadia's Farmhome.

It seems like 10 years instead of 3 or 4 can't remember when Jacob Rubin left with Mugface and the two apostles, hope all has gone well for them. My life took a turn for the worse in love, my friend showed a gradual; stronger coolness as the days went on. Now he is the aloof gladiator. He also began sending Dylan out to me from the porch with neither a good morning nor a good day.

The final straw was this precious child had to sneak away from home to come to me to say goodbye, crying and saying we are going to Rome-saw the trunks, too.

Andrew did I deserve to lose all in this earthly life, my heart is sore from crying and praying. Please let Jacob return soon with your right sandal. I will never let it be separated again, I promised.

My heart's desire too with some planning to start looking for an older small hut useable and likeable for me and for the school. I know God knows what I need.

The area should be closer to the bigger and growing community we heard are forming especially North of where we are living. This will mean more children for schooling and a chance of making their lives important no slave ring for my children ran through her mind. The school will teach the children of the villages but for an orphan will be a permanent and great place to live, yes, she would be a Mother to all of them.

Bohndan has given his blessing along with financial support. Please God answer my prayers, I need not now to dwell on the gladiator, the last time I saw him he seemed to drag his foot more. Yet it is that very image which appears in my nightly dream. I cannot help myself.

She began packing and unpacking all the while talking sort of out loud. She was glad she had hugged Dylan several times when she gave him some written work to study on his voyage.

Spec is thinking of only himself, not the child oh how could I even be attractive to such a thoughtless man. His heart is also thinking about Zeus and Rome, not Jesus.

About the Author

Pearl before leaving the farm, had three God-sky moments. One was in the mix as she overhears Earl and Chuck, planning to go to Sistler's Landing a bait store where candy is sold. Bit of honey on her mind she dresses and slips away from the house. She knew Sistler's could be reached by road and track because of the famous fisherman's path that went down the hill behind the landing which had these tracks running back of the Landing. She knew the old swimming hole was in that area, where her brothers tried to get her to swim, which never happened as they moved when she was nine.

Train routes ran back and forth crossing the old 224 road and heading for Hartville, this track cut right through the back property dividing our land. A pole was marked where hobos could get a bit to eat and mother fed many. Pearl walked on track from the time she could walk. Mother somehow always got the cows across the walk way to the pasture and back at night without a train problem.

Pearl was a tag along when her brothers went fishing. So, she knew only the track in her back yard and to the fishing hole, but the tracks crossing the road (Wingfoot) that went on over the man-made dirt bridge which had water on both sides of it. No.

The first whistle was a faint one. It was too late to turn backstill too far from the fisherman's path,-whistle loud and long-now the train was crossing Wingfoot Crossing!! What to do? Only a small gravel dirt area for her to stand-turning in circles one side-water and lily pads were higher-so went back over the track to the right side. Now she sees the Engine coming.

She then heard within herself *instructions. Lie face down as close to the ground and water put arms over your head and ears.*

She could feel heat, noise of the wheels, and air coming from under the train over her back and arms.

Finally, raising up her head and with eyes and ears, sees and hears the end car with its wobbling sound on the tracks as it went and then hears and sees the water splashing against the bank-small waves against the shore line, toward her foot-her small weight, the force of the heat and air from under the train would have knock her into the lake if she had stood.

Earl, Pearl, Chuck

Tracks Going Toward Sisler's

Going Toward Home

Pig Pen & Barn Gone

SUFFIELD

2018

PORTAGE COUNTY SCHOOLS
1942 - 1943

PRIMARY GRADES

SUFFIELD

REPORT OF

Pearl Smithern

Crystal E. Norton
TEACHER

LELAND C. KELLER
Local Superintendent

CALVIN RAUSCH
County Superintendent

PORTAGE COUNTY SCHOOLS
1943 - 1944

PRIMARY GRADES

SUFFIELD

REPORT OF

Pearl Smithern

Clara E. Day
TEACHER

DAVID C. NELSON
Local Superintendent

PORTAGE COUNTY SCHOOLS
1944 - 1945

ELEMENTARY
Grades 1-6

SUFFIELD

REPORT OF

Pearl Smithern

Alice Knapp
Teacher

DAVID C. NELSON
Local Superintendent

The Goodyear blimp, "The Spirit of Akron" cruises the skies over its home city.

Suffield Township, Portage County, Ohio

Suffield Township is one of the eighteen townships of Portage County, Ohio, United States. The 2000 census found 6,383 people in the township.[3]

Contents

Geography

Located in the southwestern corner of the county, it borders the following townships and city:

- Brimfield Township - north
- Rootstown Township - northeast corner
- Randolph Township - east
- Lake Township, Stark County - south
- Springfield Township, Summit County - west
- Tallmadge - northwest corner

Part of the village of Mogadore is located in northwestern Suffield Township.

Formed from the Connecticut Western Reserve, Suffield Township covers an area of 24 sq mi (62 km^2).

Geographical features

- Flatiron Lake Bog preserve (a 97-acre (390,000 m^2) kettle hole bog formed about 12,000 years ago; maintained by

Suffield Township

Township

Wingfoot Lake and the Goodyear Airship Hangar

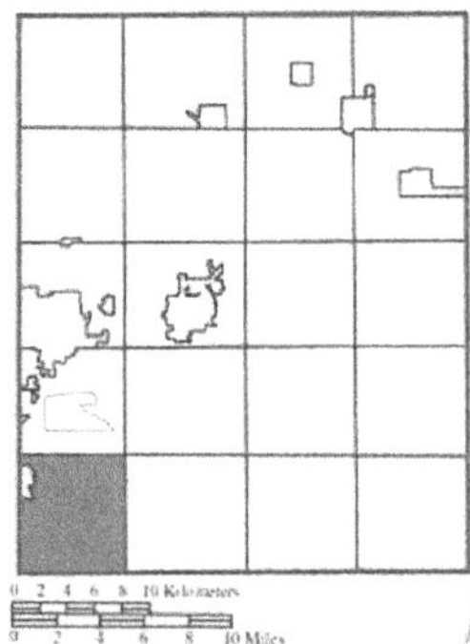

Location within Portage County

Coordinates: 41°1'40"N 81°21'1"W

Country	United States
State	Ohio

	The Nature Conservancy)[1]		
County	Portage	
Area		
• **Total**	24.7 sq mi (64.0 km^2)	
• **Land**	22.9 sq mi (59.4 km^2)	
• **Water**	1.8 sq mi (4.7 km^2)	
Elevation[1]	1,181 ft (360 m)	
Population (2000)		
• **Total**	6,383	
• **Density**	278.5/sq mi (107.5/km^2)	
Time zone	Eastern (EST) (UTC-5)	
• **Summer (DST)**	EDT (UTC-4)	
ZIP code	44260	
Area code(s)	330, 234	
FIPS code	39-75189[2]	
GNIS feature ID	1086841[1]	

(http://www.nature.org/wherewework/northamerica/states/ohio/preserves/art3092.html)

Name and history

Suffield Township was named after Suffield, Connecticut, the hometown of many its first settlers.[4] It is the only Suffield Township statewide.[5] A post office called Suffield was established in 1836, and remained in operation until 1966. In the southwestern part of the township was a settlement called **Mishler**, which had a post office from 1882 until 1917.[6]

Government

The township is governed by a three-member board of trustees, who are elected in November of odd-numbered years to a four-year term beginning on the following January 1. Two are elected in the year after the presidential election and one is elected in the year before it. There is also an elected township fiscal officer,[7] who serves a four-year term beginning on April 1 of the year after the election, which is held in November of the year before the presidential election. Vacancies in the fiscal officership or on the board of trustees are filled by the remaining trustees.

References

1. "US Board on Geographic Names" (http://geonames.usgs.gov). United States Geological Survey. 2007-10-25. Retrieved 2008-01-31.

2. "American FactFinder" (http://factfinder2.census.gov). United States Census Bureau. Retrieved 2008-01-31.

3. Portage County, Ohio — Population by Places Estimates (http://www.osuedc.org/profiles/population/places.php?sid=41&fips=39133) Ohio State University, 2007. Accessed 15 May 2007.

4. *History of Portage County, Ohio: Containing a History of the County, Its Townships, Towns, Villages, Schools, Churches, Industries, Etc* (https://books.google.com/books?id=RVDWAAAAMAAJ&pg=PA565#v=onepage&q&f=false). Warner, Beers & Company. 1885. p. 565.

5. "Detailed map of Ohio" (http://www2.census.gov/geo/maps/general_ref/cousub_outline/cen2k_pgsz/oh_cosub.pdf) (PDF). United States Census Bureau. 2000. Retrieved 2007-02-16.

6. "Portage County" (http://www.postalhistory.com/postoffices.asp?task=display&state=OH&county=Portage). Jim Forte Postal History. Retrieved 13 January 2016.

7. §503.24 (http://codes.ohio.gov/orc/503.24), §505.01 (http://codes.ohio.gov/orc/505.01), and §507.01 (http://codes.ohio.gov/orc/507.01) of the Ohio Revised Code. Accessed 4/30/2009.

External links

- County website (http://www.co.portage.oh.us)

Говорят — кур доят, а коровы яйца несут…

In Russia it is said that chickens are milked, and cows carry eggs. (A mockery of those who believe ridiculous rumors.)

This is a Ukraine Squirrel!

by *(http://windowstorussia.com/author)* | Posted on *January 29, 2014*
(http://windowstorussia.com/ukraine-this-is-ukraine-squirrel_16.html)

(http://windowstorussia.com/wp-content/uploads/2014/01/00480.jpg)

Search …   **Search**

Popular Links

Russian Churches
(http://windowstorussia.com/russian-
churches)

Recipes From Russia
(http://windowstorussia.com/recipes-from-
russia)

Permission

Permission to reprint in whole or in part is
gladly granted, provided full credit (link) is
given…

13 +

Andalusian donkey

Andalusian donkey

Other names	Asno Andaluz
	Asno Cordobés
	Asno de Lucena
Country	Spain
Origin	
Use	transport
	siring mules

Traits

Height	Male:	160 cm[1]:418
	Female:	150 cm[1]:418

Classification

APA (Spain)	Breed standard (http://www.magrama.gob.es/es/ganaderia/temas/zootecnia/Anexo_I_LG_Asnal_Andaluza_tcm7-297450.pdf)

Donkey

Equus asinus

The **Andalusian**, Spanish: **Asno Andaluz**, is a breed of domestic donkey native to the province of Córdoba in Andalusia, Spain. It is also known as the **Asno Cordobés** ("Cordovan donkey") after the city of Córdoba or the **Asno de Lucena** ("Lucena donkey")[2] because of its alleged origin in the town of Lucena, Córdoba. It is considered the oldest of the European breeds, at some 3,000 years, and today is rare.

Characteristics

The Andalusian is a large donkey, averaging 150–160 centimetres (59–63 in) at the withers and of medium length. The head is of medium size, with a convex profile; the neck is muscular. The coat is short and fine, and soft to the touch; it is pale grey, sometimes almost white. The Andalusian donkey is strong and sturdy, yet docile and calm. It is well adapted to the hot and arid conditions of its native environment.[1]:418

Status

The current state of the Andalusian breed is critical. At the end of 2013 the total population was reported at 749, of which almost all were in Andalucia.[3] Conservation plans include sparing use as work animal in the field and the forest (work which can also be done by horses), and use in rural tourism initiatives that have been followed in some places like Mijas (Málaga).

References

1. Miguel Fernández Rodríguez, Mariano Gómez Fernández, Juan Vicente Delgado Bermejo, Silvia Adán Belmonte, Miguel Jiménez Cabras (eds.) (2009). *Guía de campo de las razas autóctonas españolas* (in Spanish). Madrid: Ministerio de Medio Ambiente y Medio Rural y Marino. ISBN 9788449109461.
2. Raza equino asnal ANDALUZA (http://www.magrama.gob.es/es/ganaderia/temas/zootecnia/razas-ganaderas/razas/catalogo/peligro-extincion/equino-asnal/andaluza/default.aspx) (in Spanish). Ministerio de Agricultura, Alimentación y Medio Ambiente. Accessed May 2014.
3. Raza equino asnal ANDALUZA: Datos censales (http://www.magrama.gob.es/es/ganaderia/temas/zootecnia/razas-ganaderas/razas/catalogo/peligro-extincion/equino-asnal/andaluza/iframe-ejemplo-arca.aspx) (in Spanish). Ministerio de Agricultura, Alimentación y Medio Ambiente. Accessed May 2014.

Q: Why do donkeys bray?

A:

QUICK ANSWER

Donkeys bray to communicate with other donkeys and their owners. A donkey's bray, also referred to as a hee-haw, is unique, and each donkey sounds slightly different. CONTINUE READING

KEEP LEARNING

Can donkeys reproduce?

Where do donkeys live?

Where do donkeys come from?

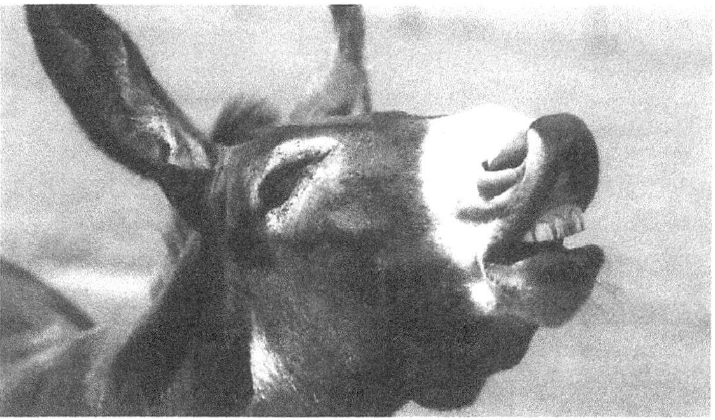

Credit: Karl Kehm / E+ / Getty Images

FULL ANSWER

Due to their distinctive and loud bray, donkeys are sometimes used as guards for livestock such as goats, sheep and calves. The guard donkey bonds with its stock and becomes aggressive if the herd is threatened. They remain alert while grazing and have a large visual range that assists with detecting predators. The donkey's bray is loud and startling to many predators and can chase them away before they do any damage. If the predator continues to advance, the donkey may charge, bite, kick or slash at it with its hooves.

LEARN MORE ABOUT BARNYARD MAMMALS

Sources: firstmaintanddonkeyandmuleclub.webs.com   motherearthnews.com

RECOMMENDED FOR YOU

Color: Luts'k

George Cohen

Christine Tkach Cohen

Jordan(Tanner) Cohen   Asher-wolf

Mischief-wolf

Tanner Cohen marries Phoebe Rubin

Color: Zhytomyr

Bohndan Tkach

Nadia Tkach

Ahava Donkey from Malka

Wandering Star from Ahava

Lesia Chin (Tkach)

Mara Chin

 Brother   Lee Chin

Wife: Acho   Son: Tan

Twins   Lilly and Lotus

Tan's wife Dia   book 3

Neighbor- Speculus

Sudano: Rome, Italy Greece, House of Claudius

Dylan (donutus)

Grandfather: Dillon Daedalus Welsh

Dogs: Bo'bik   Warrior

Horse: Pegasus Mighty wind)
Anthony Rom's - Rome

Barn: North of Kiev   School

Color: Kirovohrad

Ezar Rubin   Dell Rubin

Daughter: Phoebe Son Jacob

Horse: Grey   Old Goat

Oleg Rubin adopted book 3
Neighbor

John   and Christine

Baby boy-Andrew

Color :Donetsk

Andrew and his donkey Malka

Color: Annual Spring Sale

Shore of the Black Sea

Mykolayiv   Odessa(Tyrus)

**Color: Crimean Peninsula
Chersonesos**

Mugface   Wife: Callidora

Samuel-brother   Sister: Potamia

Children: Nicholas Jr., Lauren, Eunice, Alexis, Caity* become Mrs. Jacob Rubin

Cat: Etan

©GraphicMaps.com
200 mi
200 km
Vilnius
Lithuania
Poland
Minsk
Belarus
Desna River
Warsaw
Russia
Chernihiv
Slovakia
Luts'k
Chernobyl
Zhytomyr
Kiev
Kharkiv
L'viv
Ukraine
Dnieper River
Donets River
Luhans'k
Carpathian Mtns.
Kirovohrad
Dnipropetrovs'k
Chernivtsi
Southern Bug
Uzhhorod
Dniester River
Zaporizhzhya
Donetsk
Hungary
Chisnau
Mykolayiv
Mariupol
Moldova
Kherson
Sea of Azov
Odesa
Romania
Crimean Peninsula
Kerch
Sevastopal
Yalta
Bucharest
Black Sea
worldatlas
Bulgaria
UKRAINE
Turkey
LOW / HILLS / MOUNTAINS

How are you?
你好?
Good morning.
早安
Good afternoon
午安
Good Evening
晚安
Good bye or
see you later
再見

God bless you..
神賜福給你
Praise the LORD
讚美主
Thank you
謝 謝
PEARL
珠